# When Darkness Begins

Tina O'Hailey

Black Rose Writing | Texas

©2020 by Tina O'Hailey
All rights reserved. No part of this book may be reproduced, stored in a retrieval system or transmitted in any form or by any means without the prior written permission of the publishers, except by a reviewer who may quote brief passages in a review to be printed in a newspaper, magazine or journal.

The author grants the final approval for this literary material.

First printing

This is a work of fiction. Names, characters, businesses, places, events, and incidents are either the products of the author's imagination or used in a fictitious manner. Any resemblance to actual persons, living or dead, or actual events is purely coincidental.

ISBN: 978-1-68433-495-7
PUBLISHED BY BLACK ROSE WRITING
www.blackrosewriting.com

Printed in the United States of America
Suggested Retail Price (SRP) $18.95

*When Darkness Begins* is printed in Garamond

\*As a planet-friendly publisher, Black Rose Writing does its best to eliminate unnecessary waste to reduce paper usage and energy costs, while never compromising the reading experience. As a result, the final word count vs. page count may not meet common expectations.

# DEDICATION

To my loving family and creativity enablers:
John (Mr. O), Danny, and Joseph O'Hailey.

To my Dad: my first storytelling buddy.

# ACKNOWLEDGMENTS

This book was written thanks to the communal spirit created by NaNoWriMo (National Novel Writing Month), the Black Rose Writing Authors' Facebook group, and the Sh!tty Writers Group—even though they threaten to kick me out for getting published.

The core idea of the Vechey's three circles and what those represent came from Sherron Ostrander, the editor of the first of the Darkness Universe books: *Absolute Darkness*. She had written a short sentence in the margins, "wouldn't it be neat if." It was, indeed, neat if.

Special thanks for notes and endless support from alpha readers John O'Hailey, Dr. Denise Smith, Matt Maloney, Sherron Ostrander, and Myrna Attaway. Your honesty and patience push me forward.

Final words from the author:
I hope you enjoy *When Darkness Begins*. My confession to you is that I do not read YA and I have never read YA—even when I was of the age. I started reading not-age-appropriate books in middle school. My apologies if this isn't like other YA stories that involve high school, bullies, first-loves, lost-loves, soul-searching about what one's purpose in life is, etc. I guess this book is all of those things set in an un-modern time, with an unusual group of beings, in a touching and complex multiple-timeline story; just what I would have wanted to read when I was 16

# When Darkness Begins

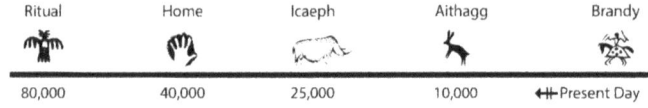

## A note about time and place:

The Vechey have no concept of time or modern day calendars. They do not live in time as we do. The timeline above represents where the story takes place as it relates to present day, *your* present day.

**Main-Time:** This represents where the "present" currently is. Though it varies, as there are scenes set in modern time, mostly the "present" is at least 9,000 years before you hold this book in your hands.

**Home-Time:** Is a place 40,000 years in the past where the Vechey's founder and leader, Eterili, has brought her tribe. They live there linearly in time like humans (or "Linears") to grow their young and prepare them for the ritual that pushes them to their individual frozen-time.

**Frozen-Time**: Each Vechey who passes through the ritual gets locked into a single moment in time. There, time stands still. They no longer experience it. Meanwhile, Main-Time (the present) continues to trudge along for the rest of the time-dwelling people (you and me).
Icaeph's frozen-time is 25,000 years in the past. Aithagg's frozen-time is 10,000 years in the past.
Vechey must move to Main-Time to feed. They protect Main-Time from being destroyed by the soul-devouring Manipulators.

**The Manipulators:** These energy beings posses the Linears and must live through time linearly. Their sole need and passion is to destroy time in a desperate attempt to find release from their hellish existence on earth. They have lost all reasoning and memory of who they once were.

**The Ritual:** While many touch points in the story are based upon archeological findings, the ritual event itself is fabricated to exist 80,000 years ago. Such events have been recorded throughout history but not necessarily in the place that I have put this one.

The setting for most of the story takes place in Tennessee and Kentucky, with travels to the ritual site, which is located in South Carolina near the Topper Site. The caves represented in the book are mostly real. The home place of the Vechey is in Mammoth Cave 40,000 years ago. Icaeph and Aithagg's cave is actually a small "cave", which is only about 35 feet long, below the mountain-bluff cabin where I live. I have composited my favorite caves into what I wish was beyond the small crawl at the back of that 35 foot opening into the mountain. This particular small walk-in-shelter "cave" is what started my fascination with dark holes in the ground.

*When Darkness Begins* is the prequel to *Absolute Darkness*. *Absolute Darkness* takes place in your present day and Alexander's time 10,000 years before today. However, given the timeline nature of this book series, this prequel also has a storyline that ties directly into *Absolute Darkness,* making it a prequel *and* a continuation. How much fun is that? You can follow this book without having read *Absolute Darkness* but to see the whole tragedy you must read about Alexander's modern day love, Brandy, and her fate in *Absolute Darkness.*

The Darkness Universe, where all of my novels reside, is a multi-verse. Major things occur and cross between the books, however, there are differences, as one would expect in a multi-verse. Certainly, it isn't because I lost track of things. It's science.

*"A ritual includes the letting of blood. Rituals which fail in this requirement are but mock rituals...Dont look away."*
*-Blood Meridian by Cormac McCarthy*

*"It's astounding - Time is fleeting.*
*Madness takes its toll."*
*-Rocky Horror Picture Show*

*The Heaviest Burden..."This life as you live it at present, and have lived it, you must live it once more, and also innumerable times; and there will be nothing new in it...and similarly this spider and this moonlight among the trees... The eternal sand-glass of existence will ever be turned once more, and you with it, you speck of dust!"*
*-Friendrich Neitzsche- the Gay Science Book IV – Aphorism #341 1882*

# 1 CIRCLES IN TIME

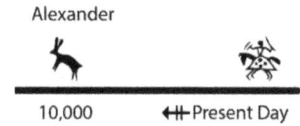

For someone who walked through time unimpeded, Alexander was bad at keeping track of it. What had Brandy called him? A time-lord?

He had confessed his true nature to her, but she was incoherent at the time: sedated and healing from being pushed under a bus by his nemesis—Yindi.

She had slurred, "Are you a time-lord, or something?" Then she fell asleep, the truth of his nature still a secret to her.

Alexander stood, unseen on the porch—wild flowers in hand, watching Brandy feed bacon to a stray orange cat. For months he hid her in the past to heal. Here the Manipulator, Yindi, would not find her. Yindi was locked in present time, 10,000 years in the future from where Alexander now stood, wild-flowers drooping in his hand. She was safe. Meanwhile, Alexander had worked tirelessly slipped back and forth through time preparing things for the coming battle with the Manipulator. Not being able to keep track of time's minutia which she experienced so inherently, he left her alone for days and weeks at a time. He brought flowers hoping to apologize for his absence.

Alexander stood in a frozen second of time, not part of the Linear time progression. He stood and watched her, afraid to sync with time and enter the inevitable confrontation with her. He feared what bearing his true nature to her would bring. Fear? Judgment? Loathing?

A smile, sad and lonely, crossed his face. 10,000 plus years ago had not his first love feared the same? Catha. She feared what their people, the Vechey, would think of her when they found out she was not developing her Vechey time-slipping skills. Instead, she was doomed to be a Linear: one who stayed trapped in time.

Linears: disparaged, shunned. Shamed for being mortal and trapped in time. Unworthy of the Vechey tribe. Unworthy to become a time-guardian and protect the world from the destruction wielded by the Manipulators. Unclean. Food for Vechey. Pawns of the universe.

Together Catha and Alexander had prepared for the Vechey coming-of-age ritual. A ritual that weeded out the unworthy. A bloody rite of passage that only the strong adolescent Vechey survived. It pushed the surviving Vechey out of time, where they would forever guard time from the Manipulators' malevolence.

The Vechey endured endless circles of existence and struggle: Linears, Vechey, Manipulators.

Alexander watched Brandy a moment longer while contemplating his first love ages ago. He had accepted Catha with his whole being. Now he understood his continual love with Linears was him looking for the same unconditional acceptance in return.

He smirked. Had he though? Did he not try to help Catha through the ritual, to be a Vechey even though she had not developed the traits? Had he not persistently insisted she be by his side? Was that for her or for him?

Alexander considered. Perhaps he continually fell for Linears to deny himself long lasting companionship, to torture himself for failing Catha.

Perhaps.

Eterili, the clan's leader, had called him out on it once when he was young, when he was Aithagg. She knew. She knew all.

He stepped into time, flowers in hand, and approached Brandy. He hoped he would not fail her as he had Catha. Maybe he was only trying to atone for his teenage mistakes 10,000 years ago.

# 2 THE END

The last thought that rambled through Eterili's ancient skull was a mixture of relief and understanding. She smiled because at last the nature of the universe was clear to her. It did not stay; it built up. Tore apart. Built up somewhere else. Tore apart again. To her it was like a vessel filled with water. Empty the vessel into multiple cups. In turn, pour those cups into yet other vessels. That was how the universes were to her. Souls and energy poured from one place to another, taking shape here or there, moving and flowing constantly over the eons.

Darkness fell across the sun. The surrounding air seemed to dim as the shadows cast upon the ground became soft and distorted.

Her last breath, for she did breathe air unlike most Vechey, released in a silent shudder.

The sun sunk into itself and imploded, destroying all in its path. The energy it expelled pushed all Vechey, including Eterili, through time and into the next plane where they would begin again.

The darkness signaled the end of this universe—which had grown and stretched until the sky was void of stars. It was a homecoming.

Eterili smiled. It was good.

# 3 THE BEGINNING

The tree would fall. There was no mistaking it held its last grip of the earth. The ground tried in vain to hold the struggling roots. Birds feasted on the grubs that made a home of its bark. Squirrels, large and fat, gathered its final pinecones and nestled in its branches. It reached its needle-covered branches to the sky in one last attempt to reach something. It wasn't sure what it reached for. Something it missed? Something that was there? It did not remember. Its dying needles no longer sensed the warmth of the sun to remind it. The moisture from the morning's dew shook in fine droplets to the ground. The grass underneath the tree soaked up the water droplets greedily. They flattened their blades to the sky offering more surfaces for water to funnel into their stalks. Their root system tunneled through the ground and weaved around the tree.

A gentle wind blew. Clouds parted and gave way to a deep blue sky. The sun burned off the morning fog and marched towards its zenith. It cast reflections in a nearby pond that danced and sparkled.

A lone leaf floated on the water. A small ladybug, dark red with uneven brown spots, walked the edge of the leaf—continually in a circle, never knowing it was repeating its same track.

The air was cool but not as chilled as it had been eons before. The ice had retreated and now the rains fell. Grass grew. Trees tried to reach the clouds without remembering why.

Eterili stood beside the tree and placed a comforting hand upon it. She bade it a good journey and watched as it fell pulling its roots from the ground. Its energy released, dissipating into the rest of the energy that was the world and the universe beyond. It was good.

She was an old woman, even now. She had survived growing up with Linears not by chance, but by sheer wit. Even in the womb she had known she was different. She was not as the Linears. She had opened her eyes in a utero-darkness and listened to the world, the surrounding universe. Linears, even the woman that birthed her, did not see the things she saw nor hear the things she heard. They did not have memories of lives before as she did. They had not seen the universe die and be re-born countless times as she had.

The incalculable times she had been born and lived were acts of patience and endurance. Seeing much. Waiting to move. Knowing an end would come only to begin again, finding no release from the tedium.

She had been one with the sand, the trees, the air, while the planet formed and life inhabited it. Much like the tree had yearned to touch the sky and the vastness beyond—she too had yearned when she was nothing more than particles scattered across snow-capped mountains: conscious, aware, remembering all.

Eventually the particles that were her gathered into a raindrop, a mist, or the morning dew, and would come closer to the bipeds of the world. This gathering was not conscious—it occurred—and she had stopped trying to control that aspect of her existence thousands of rotations ago. Eventually she would awake in an embryotic stasis not knowing how she came to be there.

Then countless times she had been born to a woman and lived as long as the universe did, moving through time and learning all there was. The universe would extinguish in an eruption of fury and she would lay wait, another element adrift in the vastness, until she took form again.

The eve before the universe collapsed this latest time, Eterili headed the signs and considered her choices. She had moved through the universe alone, time and time again. The loneliness weighed heavily on her this particular rotation. What if she did not go through this alone? She pondered.

The lands she had inhabited nearly all followed along a similar path. The upright-biped species emerged, fought for food, died out, eventually a people would survive. They would begin vocalizing, communicating, developing. Tools followed. Control of the elements such as metals came soon after. Information exchange and language. War. Expansion. Religion. Factions. Agriculture. Science. Revolutions. Curiosity. Arts. Industrialism. Technology. Exploring.

War, collapse, rebuilding—a constant interruption in any part of the ritual.

Why had she always chosen to be alone?

Eterili had a singular skill that the Linears did not have. She was a time-walker, able to move into times past of this universe and see far into the future. See, but not visit those times yet to come. Linears had stoned her to mortal death the first time she exhibited this skill. Scattered to the winds, as a moldy corpse does, she had to await the inevitable collapse of the universe to begin again. The interminable boredom of waiting with an inability to do anything stung mightily.

She was able to die, as evidenced by her stoning, yet it only killed the body she had been born to. The only way to kill her physical body, she had found, was by a severing of the spine. Even the gravest of injuries would re-heal, though not without excruciating pain. Each death she would lie awake as part of the ground awaiting re-birth. Many times she lived as long as the universe. As many times she died a true death early, sometimes by pure accident, other times out of boredom and frustration.

In future lives, after her stoning, she was much more careful to explore her abilities in solitude and removed herself as soon as possible from Linears. Perhaps she had chosen solitude as a matter of survival and maintained the choice out of habit, a very long-standing habit.

As she explored her strengths and unusual gifts more, Eterili pushed into the past as far as the beginning of the universe's timeline, even when she herself had been only a collection of snow on a mountaintop. However, she was unable to move into the future, as that time did not exist yet. Each collapse and rebirth of the universe and herself issued another boundary to move within.

At first, when the universe was young and she new to it, she had not found time-walking useful. When she realized moving and adjusting time would ultimately adjust the course of the universe itself, it intrigued her. Rebellious in her youth, she had adjusted events and caused the collapse of the universe herself many times. The power was intoxicating, but she eventually grew tired of it.

What if she adjusted time, adjust things, made herself the ruler of this universe and not merely be a hapless spectator enslaved to constant existence thrown against the shores of time by meaningless chaos?

The sky had grown dark, and she knew the end of the universe was moments away. Set upon her plan to wield the cosmos to her desires—she waited her next becoming.

# 4 NEW BEGINNINGS

In a freezing and distant land, Eterili's mother had hidden her as a baby from the others of the clan. They would have torn her to pieces and fed her to the wolves if they had heard the inhuman words that came from her mouth.

Even as she suckled, she spoke. Not the cooing of a baby but every language known and most not known. Her mother held the child at arm's length when she had uttered her first words.

Not one word. A sentence.

The child had simply spat out the teat it fed from and proclaimed, "Today, I am."

Though the voice was soft and hardly shaped, the words were unmistakable. Most of the mother's clan barely spoke words or grunts let alone utter multiple words strung together. The mother thought more abstractly and hid the fact well lest she be exiled from the clan. She hid her thoughts adeptly. Her child, however, was speaking in a language she did not quite understand but knew it had meaning.

Though she still bled from the difficult birthing, the mother joined a hunting party and headed north with them, taking the child with her. She traveled quickly and bade the child to keep quiet during their journey, fearing they would be found out and killed. The child seemed to understand and kept quiet.

In the stillness of their makeshift tent at night, the child taught the mother words and languages. The mother struggled with it and thought she was becoming insane. She could not deny her child, so tried with all of her might to learn no matter how impossible it might seem to her.

They traveled for moons and the child grew. The child's hair was black as night and her eyes were gray as a wolf's fur. She listened to her mother and together they avoided detection. By the time the youngster was walking, a few of the hunting party had died horrible, unexplainable deaths. The mother and child stayed at the edges of the clan and kept to themselves. The hunters cast wary eyes at them and offered no aid save allowing them near the fire. Suspicions grew when the clan found another hunter with his throat slashed and a disproportionally small bloodstain upon the snow. Even the meager hospitality of the fire would soon be withheld from the outcast mother and child.

The night was cold. While crossing a large expanse of ice, wolves attacked the hunting party. The child, still young and unable to keep up with the group, stayed in a papoose on her mother's back. The mother kept her back towards the clansmen as they fought the wolves.

One wolf jumped and took down a clansman closest to the child. It snarled and bit, dispatching the man in a vicious twist of its mighty head. It glared at the toddler and bared its teeth.

One by one, the wolves rendered the clansman useless until only the mother stood, the toddler on her back.

The wolves closed in until the pack surrounded the two.

Mother twisted and pulled the papoose around to hold her baby in her arms, a protective gesture, the last she thought she would have.

Snow fell on the group, dusting her eyelashes and the wolves' backs equally. No one moved. Only silence and the sounds of wolves growling filled the air. The baby did not cry. The mother held her sobs for they would do no good now. She waited for death.

She waited.

Snow fell.

She waited with eyes wide open.

Only snow fell.

The wolves sat around her as if awaiting a command. She marveled at it with her mouth agape. It was then she noticed the hand of her baby extended from the papoose. Not a feebly waving limb but an upheld hand in the gesture of a command.

The wolves put their heads on their paws and growled no more.

For the rest of their journey, the wolf pack accompanied them—sharing their half consumed kills, treating the mother and child as pups. Eventually they made their way to a cold cave far to the north. The mother built up ice chunks around the entrance of the cave to keep the wind from rushing in and to help keep the fire's warmth from escaping. There she rested. While she slept, the toddler spoke to the wolves.

The baby grew and survived. She took the name she had held since her first death: Eterili. She slept, sometimes for centuries, in the ice-cave with her mother's blood-drained corpse. Other times she sat and listened.

Isolated. Confined. Disconnected.

Waiting.

Then the ice began to recede and she heard other voices calling out: an insistent murmur.

She had not heard this before in any of her lives. Perhaps she had never listened. Perhaps in her previous life, her own dying wishes for others of her own had made it so in this universe, on this planet at least. Eterili pondered at the stars above her, not for the first time, and wondered if she would ever visit other planets and if there were others like her out there. She listened—

but heard nothing beyond the whispers from this planet. It spoke to her in a deafening roar.

The rocks called to Eterili and led her to a faraway land. She heard the rocks as clearly as the wolves and trees. They spoke in a language sensed, heard, and tasted. The whispered tidings breezed across her skin and pulled her this way and that. She followed the whispers alone in the darkness.

It took a thousand patient seasons or more to cross the lands, the sea, and the rivers to come to this new and enormous cave—a dark opening in the side of a mountain on a distant land.

The damp cave went on forever, it seemed, with its multiple entrances spread out like abscesses across the hill-stained land.

She stood at one of the entrances, and looked in. The darkness beyond was no match for her eyes. Eterili clearly saw the shapes of things now, then, and soon to become. She chose her steps wisely and made her way through the rock opening.

The prodigious passage was wide enough to hold twenty great, hairy, tusked beasts shoulder-to-shoulder. Still, their dark-furred hides would not have touched the rock walls.

Fireflies flew in front of her and lit the path at her bidding. She did not need them; it was an old woman's vanity to call them to her side.

Water trickled its way from the ceiling, dripping down calcite stone-point formations and falling into the mud below. The path of the water left mineral traces adding to the length of the stone-points. Through the ages she saw where they would grow and become walls of stone, blocking passage in future times. Perfect. This would be the home of her people.

She had to find them first. She knew they were there: others like her. Though she did not think they were as strong as her. This was new. They had not been there in previous lives. They were now. She would unite them. It would take work on her part to push events, and call to them. She would create a safe place for them to grow as a people, ensure their survival, and use them to help keep their clan together safe. This clan would become tied into this universe so they themselves could push forward into the next universe—together—where she would begin anew rebuilding her people. She would no longer be alone.

She waited and time rolled by at its plodding pace. Eterili wandered the lands and watched the Linears come to the flatlands at first in small fits and starts and then in numbers. She had seen this progress of inhabitation hundreds of thousands of times.

Carefully she walked through time calling to her people across the water and in faraway lands. She walked back through time away from the Linears and their inhabitance of the land to a time when only she had stood, a solitary figure. This time—she considered it home-time—existed far in the past from where the Linears existed, far from their intrusion. She called her people here. The strong would prevail and the time-walkers would find her in this solitude. Here they would be safe. Here they would grow, strengthen, evolve.

Standing in this cold, tremendous cave, far in the past—safe from Linear's discovery, Eterili peered through the future as it would unfold. She observed where parts of the cave stayed open for would-be adventurers to travel through. The rock would grow and protect all her people would carve and make as their home. None would find evidence of their existence. The earth would swallow their home whole as it grew its rock walls and separated their living areas from any access to the outside world.

She listened. They heard her call. Eterili smiled, sensing them, hearing them, as they moved towards here across the lands and across time; their movements louder than the rocks that called her here.

From a small pouch at her waist she chose iron tools. These tools didn't exist yet on this planet, but soon would if it followed as her experience had seen in previous lives. Hefting a small axe in one hand and using a rock as a hammer in the other she began carving into the stone. It took time, and she reveled in inscribing designs for each family branch that would join her. As if by her own invention each clan became more real to her with every pounding of the rock hammer.

This was her timeline and she would wield it. She imagined the time-walkers emerged from the chaos of the universe by her own will. The shape of them took form in her mind. They would form families, clans.

With a clink she chipped away at the stone and carved. The designs were intricate, and she lost herself in them for months.

At last she decided that she would name her people Vechey. Eterili put away her tools and looked at her work. She had toiled for years to prepare this place. It awaited them.

The full moon greeted her when she exited the cave. It was an old friend, and she spoke to him gently, "We will call the Vechey to join us here from wherever they have appeared. They must come home."

Pausing, she looked up at the luminous orb above her. This was only the start. There was one more thing to do. She had to help her Vechey escape time as she had, enabling them to move forward with her when this universe ended.

The stars filled the night sky and again Eterili pondered on what her next steps might be. A meteor shower streaked across the sky and for a moment the moon's brightness competed with the red and orange stripes across the black void. The meteors spoke to her even as they burned to their death in the upper atmosphere, leaving only charred dust and elements to fall to the ground.

Nothing more than how I start my existence in each universe, Eterili thought. She thought more on space and time and how to help her people escape time's linear hold. Her plan came into place. She watched the sun rise and set—repeatedly chasing the moon until he fled the night's sky completely. The night was dark and moonless when she nodded to herself contently.

She sat, her thin legs and frame wrapped in a coyote fur. The coyote's head, eyes replaced with quartz, lolled at her shoulder. It whispered to her of endless ends and beginnings saying, "It is the way of the universe."

She smiled, "It is the way of *my* universe."

Eterili waited.

\*\*\*

The first to hear Eterili's call was a stooped man, ostracized from his tribe. He had lived long enough to see the tribe migrate away and their children migrate back. His lands of origin were even further away than where Eterili had hid with her mother in an ice-cave so long ago.

He did not have much language capacity to communicate, but the calls to him from Eterili crept into his dreams at night. In the dreams he saw a symbol carved on a rock wall: three overlapping circles. He carved them on a shell and hung it from his neck as if to ward off the dreams—to no avail.

Some of those that migrated back joined him and recognized the symbol around his neck from their dreams. Together they moved away from the tribe. They continued traveling across the lands and to the east. They encountered other tribes. Some were welcoming. Some not.

He and his small clan came across a group on an island that was so much shorter than he. They exchanged bead necklaces, and he showed them the axe he had made. It was very large.

He found more who had heard Eterili, not many, but a few along his path did.

By the time they crossed the shallow water, which burned their feet, and arrived at a large island—his tribe had grown to over seventy-five. All were outcasts from their tribes.

Different. Odd. They did not age the same. They tended to not hunt as much with the others. They walked across time in a limited fashion but had learned quickly to hide their talents.

Instinctively they separated from the Linear tribes and clumped together, moving and migrating to their own parts of the land.

Eterili called to them in their dreams. If they ignored her call the very rock and ground they slept upon whispered to them. Her unrelenting call bade them to move.

The stooped man, who had gathered a large group with him—including a handful from the tribe who were so short they looked like children, looked to his cobbled together tribe.

In a few words and gesturing, they made a plan.

Had everyone heard the calling of this distant woman called Eterili?

They had.

Her insistent cries told of a safe place for all of their kind. Did they believe it?

They did.

She proclaimed they would grow into a new group, a strong tribe. Different and united.

Yes.

The journey would be long and difficult. Across water.

Yes.

Across time.

Yes.

She vows she will teach them the ways of who they are: the Vechey.

We go.

The tribe went. From all corners of the earth small groups, much like the stooped man's group, worked together to travel across the lands, built boats to hop from island to island, moved tirelessly until they found the dry lands that would lead them towards Eterili.

It took nearly a thousand moons. They aged considerably during the trip and not all arrived to the new shore, having died along the way. They came from all times and as if drawn together by a current. They found each other as they walked across the forbidding terrain. The Vechey united on the long journey and helped each other find their way, for there were those among them unable to see through time well. Eventually, they came as one to the place and time Eterili had carved for them eons before the Linears would inhabit the lands.

She stood waiting for them, arms held wide in a welcoming gesture.

"You have arrived!" she shouted triumphantly. "Vechey! We come here to our home."

They did not understand her words but understood the meaning. Groups came in one after the other through all hours of the day and night. They settled in and made their home.

The first generation of Vechey helped continue to carve and prepare the cave rock for the next generations. Their lifespan was shorter than future Vechey. Eterili established burial rites which would put the bodies of the first generation in a sacred place deep inside of the cave that even the Vechey of future generations would not find.

She introduced rituals and doctrine. It unified the Vechey even more and served her purposes well.

It took ten generations before the first Vechey started showing the ability to walk through large time spans. There were trades offs with being able to see so much time; it was true.

Eterili continued to call to other groups as time resiliently moved forward and the Vechey remained hidden in the past.

New Vechey arrived sporadically. Some came alone. Some came with one or two. The groups were never more than a handful. Eterili weeded and manipulated time to push the correct Vechey together so the traits would strengthen and after not too long the Vechey were what she desired. They filled the cave halls and a community of Vechey, strong Vechey, filled with tradition and rituals took shape.

Eterili smiled. It was good.

# 5 HOME

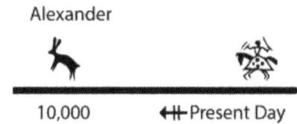

Alexander stood alone. Dead air, still and soundless, pressed in on him; Alexander took no notice. He bent to his task with a singular dedication.

Pausing his pale hands, he glanced at the blueprints once more. Dark locks fell slowly into his eyes. He pushed them away with the back of his forearm. Confident in the blueprint's direction, Alexander busied his hands again measuring the length of wood. He produced a grease pencil from his pocket and drew a dark line across the yellow timber. The graphite moved soundlessly.

A dark lock sunk again to impair his vision; malevolent follicles. Alexander stood and examined his handy work while retying the rawhide string that bound his hair. Not for the first time in ten thousand years he wondered if existence would be better if he cut off the curly mass. The answer had remained the same: it would exasperatingly grow back when he was in main-time. He would get a respite of forty years or more before he had to return to main-time and eat substantial food. He could avoid feeding for forty years if he had fed and rested well prior:

something he had not done for the past hundred or more years. His hair would not grow while here in this moment, his frozen place where time stood still. Frozen. All. Except for him. He tugged again on the rawhide to tighten the knot.

Alexander hesitated. How long had he been here working on this project? How many hours had passed in the Linear's time? He was not sure. He bent again to his task. It didn't really matter as long as he returned to Main-Time close to where he had left. His mind wandered, remembering when he had left that Linear timeline; remembering *whom* he had left in that Linear timeline: Brandy. He would return to her shortly. He smiled absently. The flowers were not going to be enough to soften the blow of what he needed to tell her. He needed something else.

All around him candles blazed, their flames frozen and unmoving. Shadows cast by the light lingered in eerie stillness and did not follow Alexander as he moved.

He picked up a saw, placed the sharp steel to the wood, and began rhythmically drawing the serrated blade. His strength aided the cut and made short work of it. Gravity had less effect in this frozen moment: the freed length of wood drifted slowly towards the ground. Alexander absently brushed the sawdust from the plank and from his movement the sawdust skittered through time both forward and back.

The lock crept into his vision again. He ignored it and took the plank towards the room he was building. Alexander's thin lips parted into a smile. What a surprise this would be for his…

What to call this relationship that might last only a few Linear months? This unnatural relationship. Did he love her only because he wanted to protect her? Was that the reason he returned again and again to love—those unlike him? *Linears*: beings forced to live in time. Their lives desperately short, unlike his nearly immortal existence. Linears: those who should be his sustenance. He brushed the thought aside like sawdust. His face flushed with shame and then darkened with sadness.

Alexander returned to the table intent on cutting another plank of wood. The silence and stillness was more like home to him than anything. Thousands of years in silence had not rendered him mad, though, his ancestors had warned him madness crept in unnoticed through the millennia. Many of his kind had been lost to it, suffering horrible deaths. Their bodies discovered lifeless and stilled with gaping eye sockets—bloody where they had clawed out their eyes with their own gnarled hands.

He held out his own hand before him: smooth and young. No madness here, he thought to himself reassuringly. If derangement stole in unnoticed, how would one know?

Alexander took in a deep breath as if to smell the wood, but breathed only dead air. Smells did not dissipate for one's enjoyment without time to aid their travel. He frowned and dismissed the desire to enjoy the scent. It had been a favorite smell in his childhood, thousands of years ago. It harked back to creating valuable things for the family. His mind drifted as he stacked an inhuman number of planks into his arms. The wood pinched at his flesh. He did not notice.

# 6 HOME BEFORE

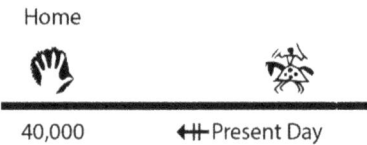

"Do you know all the answers, Father?" Young Aithagg sat on the tree stump, his legs swinging back and forth. Occasionally he would dip a foot down to stir the leaves. Dirt and leaves bounded from his invasive big toe.

The tall man straightened and chuckled. "Aithagg, I do not even know all the questions." He spit into each hand, grabbed new purchase on a large rock and chopped again at the tree he bent at. The sharpened edge bit at the bark, splinters fell to the ground with each blow.

The youth, five years old, watched with curious eyes. He cocked his head to one side; wavy locks fell in front of his eyes. He blinked to see through them. "How do you find all the questions?"

The reply came between blows of the rock cutting the tree.
THUMP
"You keep—"
THUMP
"—asking—"

THUMP

"—more questions—"

THUMP

"—to find new—"

THUMP. CRACK.

"—questions."

The tree fell to the ground. Its girth made a solid smacking sound as it hit the compacted dirt. The flickering torch nearby cast eerie highlights on the fallen timber.

His father continued, "You do not always find the answers." He bent at the knee and faced the youngster. "Or the answers are not the ones you wanted."

Aithagg jumped down from the stump and touched the fresh cut at the base of the tree. His hands came away sticky with sap. The boy held his fingers together and pulled them apart, mesmerized by how the skin stuck at the finger pads. He turned his fingers towards the light to see better in the darkness.

"It is not always that way. You often find answers you knew were there all along but were unable to see." The man took the young boy's sticky hand in his. "You will need to go back and wash before the meal."

Aithagg pouted and harrumphed, "I want to help take the bark off."

"Go now and wash. We have much to do and you need to learn patience. There is plenty of time to help with stripping bark." The man watched the boy intently as if seeing more than the boy in front of him.

Aithagg considered his options and then ventured, "I promise to be very good at the circle if you let me help take the bark off."

"You'll be very good at the circle even if you do not help with the bark," the father warned.

Aithagg seemed to consider this. His eyebrows creased, and he frowned deeply.

The father watched the boy intently, again, as if seeing more than the boy in front of him. He smiled, as Aithagg stood straighter, having decided.

"I will fall my own tree and remove the bark myself tomorrow. You can watch me," Aithagg proclaimed.

"Indeed," his father responded.

The wind blew at their faces. In unison both turned into the breeze. The father continued, "We must accomplish much in the little time that we have."

Aithagg jumped onto the fallen tree and balanced, arms outstretched and wobbling. "I think Eterili smells funny."

"Go. Wash. Dinner. Then, we will gather at the circle." Playfully, he held a finger out towards Aithagg, threatening to push him off balance.

Both stared at each other, eyes locked.

Aithagg giggled.

The man feigned pushing him. Aithagg flinched and fell off the tree, landing ungracefully on the ground.

"No fair," he called. His cry dissolved into a burst of giggles as the father showered him with leaves. Aithagg held his arms up to ward off the deluge of brown foliage.

"*You* will smell funny if you do not go wash before eating," chided the father. "And your mother will *never* let me hear the end of it. Do you know how long eternity is?"

Aithagg bounded from the ground and ran at break-neck speed into the darkness.

"Last one there," his voice trailed off as he ran away from his father.

The man watched the boy run. When he had disappeared from sight, the father turned back towards the tree. He placed a hand upon the trunk and for a moment stood completely still.

Nothing moved.

The wind did not stir.

Then the surrounding air wavered and he and the tree disappeared. A popping sound rang out as the air collapsed into where he had stood.

Birds nearby, startled, took flight.

Moments later, the man and the tree reappeared. Leaves rustled away from him with a rush of wind, while some leaves stuck to the naked white gleaming wood—still fresh with sap.

\*\*\*

Over two hundred gathered at the fire circle. The flames danced and sparks flew towards the sky.

Youngsters, ignoring the warnings of their parents, dared each other to get closer to the fire, testing their ability to brave the heat.

The adolescents of the group sat closer to their parents and feigned indifference to the youngsters and elders alike, wearing attitudes of maturity like ill-fitting clothes.

The elders of the group were of youthful appearance and busy keeping watchful eyes on their young.

All silenced when the jingle of Eterili's anklets sounded her approach. She did not need to call for the attention of the crowd. All eyes were upon Eterili as she neared the fire.

The youngsters scurried to hide in their mother's arms. They ogled at the anklets of long teeth around Eterili's ankle. The anklets jangled and clattered disturbingly with every movement she made. Long teeth, canine fangs, clacked in a horrific reverberation.

She stood still, her clouded eyes transfixed on the full moon above them. Minutes passed, and the children began to fidget. The adults did not move. They waited most patiently.

Finally Eterili spoke, "I, daughter of the first, mother of all; who has traveled across the land before it split, who slept in the depths while the earth froze, who stays with time and not with time, who called to you tens of thousands of winters ago and led you to this home."

The firelight made the creases, which scoured her cheeks, stand out starkly—cracks as deep as rivers. The dirt on her feet and body clung to her in clumps. She moved slightly and came near a young child, 10 winters of age, sitting smartly next to her mother. As Eterili neared, the young girl wrinkled her nose from the smell and tried to hide it with a demure hand. The child's eyes flicked to see if her mother had noticed.

Eterili continued, "You traveled to the land that touched the sea and then crossed the marsh lands into the steep hills until we found this home." She raised her hands towards the sky as if to include the universe into the definition of home.

"Here." She lowered her hands to her side. The matted furs of questionable origination, which made up her clothing, stuck to her hands when she raised her arms, then plucked away. "Now." A pause. "For eternity."

Eyes followed as she walked around the edge of the fire, her captured audience. "We will send those that have come of age to the ritual ground where they will begin their journey. When the sun sets and the energy has faded from the sky. We. Will. Go."

Aithagg sat in front of Eterili, his eyes wide with awe. She spoke again, seemingly directly to him, "Not all will survive the ritual. Do not mourn their passing. It is an easier death to end quickly than to be separated from all you love and locked into time."

She looked again at the moon as if in deep contemplation. No one interrupted her reverie.

"You can not understand eternity given your glimpse of it now and the quickness of your growth." She stamped her feet in agitation. "You can not understand eternity. It is a weight that stretches one to nothingness if you do not keep yourself safe from it." She grabbed a stick from the fire, quicker than a woman of her age should, and spun in circles dramatically pointing the flames at the older children. "You! Kephos, Rtun, and you, Ehasa. You! Arske. Ar'mac. Phot." The smoke trailed towards each youth as if summoned. "You must listen to the teachings. Our time to teach you is a blink of the eye. You MUST carry these teachings with you else suffer staying in time like a *Linear*," she spat the word with disgust. "Come forward those that are brave enough to go through the ritual." Eterili lowered her voice into a guttural growl, "Come *forward!*"

The six adolescent youths stood—some bravely, some timidly—and walked towards Eterili. The crowd shifted. The air filled with murmurs; whispers between children, reassurances from one spouse to another, remembrances from the elders.

"Take your place at the circle with me," said Eterili.

Each youth assembled as told and faced the crowd, their backs to the warm fire.

"Your father and mother before you stood at this very circle with me. Take solace in that they went through the ritual thousands of winters ago and returned to here and now to begat you—who will now go through the same ritual. It is the way."

The crowd shifted on the ground. Most sat cross-legged on hides. Some sat on large rocks or logs brought for the occasion.

Aithagg turned towards his father, who stood behind him, a protective hand upon his shoulder. "When do I do this, Father? When do I go through the ritual?"

His father patted Aithagg's shoulder. "All too soon."

"How many do not survive?" Aithagg's voice was a whisper but carried across the crowd with the wind.

The six youths eyed each other warily; some cast their faces to the ground. One of the tallest boys puffed his chest out in defiance. Eterili looked towards Aithagg and raised an eyebrow as a warning.

He quieted. His father squeezed Aithagg's shoulder reassuringly.

Eterili continued, "You will return to the circle and watch your own offspring stand before you and proclaim their pledge to the moon and sky." The stick, once ablaze, had dwindled to a red smolder. She threw it back into the pyre. It lie still for a moment then caught fire again. "What do you pledge to me, to the moon, to the sky, to your tribe?" She squatted and stilled.

The six youths each straightened and in unison, or near it, began to articulate, "I will go forth and find my time, my place, my home. Turning away from my family and my friends, I will dedicate my eternity to keeping the universe whole. Should another adjust my time, my place, my home I will defend it until my last thought, through all eternity."

Eterili called from her squatted position, "What do you protect?"

"Time." The answer—cracking adolescent voices.

"Why?" An aged croak.

"Lest the sky pull my bones apart as the tribe is lost across all of time." Whispers.

"Who do you protect time from?"

"The Manipulators who would destroy time, the universe, and all in it."

"Yes. The Manipulators live in the skin of Linears. Your Manipulator will taunt you and try to wear *your* skin. A fate worse than madness."

"We will protect time from our Manipulator."

"Why do you each have a Manipulator?"

"The universe balances good and bad, right and wrong, Vechey and Manipulator, Linears and Vechey."

"Will you survive the ritual?" Eterili raised her eyes to look at the group.

In unison, they hesitated then answered, "If I heed my teachings, we will survive the ritual."

"It is the way," Eterili answered then tried to stand. Her knees locked and refused to budge. She grunted. Someone stood to aid her but stilled when they saw Eterili's quick glare. With a heave she stood and steadied herself; anklets clacked in protest.

A large and old Vechey male stood from the crowd and began to blow into a horn made from a massive tusk. The crowd gave a battle cry and stood, raising their fists to the sky.

Aithagg marveled at the unusually boisterous display; his eyes as round as the full moon.

\*\*\*

"Is she really as old as dirt?" Aithagg asked. His father stood over him, tucking him into bed. The first rays of sunlight had crept up over the horizon as the tribe funneled into the cave entrance, seeking the depths and the dark.

His father chuckled and said, "Who said that?"

"*She* did." Aithagg snuggled into the bedding until only his curls and the tops of his eyebrows peeked out. He raised his head slightly so his mouth poked out of the covers briefly. "She wouldn't let me touch her teeth anklets."

"Do you know what those are from?" His father sat back and patted Aithagg's chest.

"No. Who are they?" Aithagg whispered.

"The mad," Father whispered a reply.

"Like angry?" Aithagg pulled the furs down from his face, eyes at full attention.

"No, not angry. Crazy with madness. Lost from now." He patted at Aithagg's chest again. "It happens with the elders who can not stand eternity."

"How does she get their teeth? Do they pull them out when they are mad?" The youngster held his hands over his mouth.

"Some say Eterili finds them and takes them. Others say the teeth crawl back to her, she is mother of all and even our teeth must return to her." Father looked away from the youngster and gazed towards the rock wall of the room. "The sun is coming up soon. I need to rest." He stood and pulled the covers back to Aithagg's chin. "You too."

They said their goodnights and Aithagg drifted off to sleep filled with fitful dreams of teeth crawling across the rock floor to scratch at the wall.

\*\*\*

Iskeho, Aithagg's father, walked quietly through the passage. The cave walls were close but not such to cause him to stoop. The coolness did not bother him as it did the children. He walked until he came to his chamber, a domed room; here he stooped slightly to enter the roughly circular room. The ceiling, 20-foot overhead, had a small opening not even large enough for a mouse. From the mouth of the opening, a long sheet of limestone hung like frozen drapery. It glistened with moisture.

"It does not get easier, this flash of time where we grow them, teach them and then, what, shove them out into the universe and expect them to know it all?" She sat with her back to him. Her voice was a whisper.

His wife: Kei-tha. From the angle of her back he knew she was worrying a piece of something in her lap. She would turn the fabric or stone or claw over and over in her hand until it turned smooth or disintegrated from her abuse.

"Why can it not be different?" She turned to him, eyes blazing, and then continued, "Why can we not let them sync with their time and then go there and teach them properly? Watch them grow, be a part of one another's lives?"

Iskeho paused in the entryway and looked at their bare makeshift room. This time, this place, was not theirs. They had formed their union thousands of years ago and lived together synced to another time in another part of the world. They returned to this place to raise their young.

This place. He looked around again at the domed rock-walled room, deep inside the cave system which was longer than many rivers. Their room was one of a hundred such rooms spread out through the vast network of passages caused by rivers of water that had once flown through the limestone rock, when the ice had melted and Eterili had slept under the earth. He did not speak, only sat on the straw bed near his wife.

She leaned her back against his. "I do not care that it is the way," she whispered. "We should find a new way."

"Quiet woman. You speak against the tribe with this." Iskeho pulled at a burr irritating his leg. "Though I do not care for the dirt and grime that sticks when synced with time." He worried the bur with a fingernail until it dislodged.

"You should bathe. I dislike the dirt." She turned and kissed his shoulder gently. "My soul, I fear for him."

Iskeho turned his head to kiss the top of hers and silenced her. "He will survive. It will not be like the others. He will survive. Almost all of our children survived the ritual. Focus not on the few we lost."

They did not speak again as they prepared to rest. Each lay back upon their straw mat, closed their eyes, fell to sleep, and disappeared.

\*\*\*

The next evening the sun had set and the small ones had been fed. Kei-tha stood with Aithagg at the edge of the circle. The fire had not been built for the evening yet. The previous evening's fire still smoldered. No hint of worry or emotion from the previous evening marked her face. However, the rock hidden in her smock's pocket testified to her concerns; she had worked it nearly smooth with her worried hands. She stood strongly, arms at her side, feet at shoulder width. Her long, wild hair fell in raven black rivulets of curls around her angular face. Coal eyes blazed.

"We have gathered at this circle since Eterili first led us from the lands that touch the sea, thousands of winters before this time. We stand here, now, in this home-time. The universe moves forward and carries with it the time stream where Linears are trapped to sync and die in their short fashion. You and I are in time like Linears right now. Though we are in the past. One day you will be able to remove yourself from time and move to any other times that you can see. Today we practice seeing."

"Mother," Aithagg whined.

"Do not interrupt, Aithagg." Her voice was stern but loving. "I want you to practice with me before you go with the others for today's lessons."

"Catha does not have to do extra lessons," Aithagg pouted under his breath. "With her mom," he added.

"Shush now," she warned. "Now look here at the smoldering fire."

Aithagg focused on the fire as told.

"You can see the smoldering sticks as they are now. Look closely and let your thoughts open. Can you see the fire as it was last night?" Kei-tha pointed to the edge of the ash. "There, the stick that Eterili threw back into the fire. It had burst into flame and was consumed. Can you see it?"

Aithagg squinted and sighed. Disappointed he said, "I do not see it. Only now."

"Keep looking. It will eventually be as easy as blinking your eyes. For now, think about what you saw last night then look for it in front of you." She walked to the other side of the fire and sat down on a log. "Remember, I sat here." She stood and moved away from the log. "Look, can you see me sitting there last night?"

Aithagg squinted again and then relaxed his gaze. "Oh, but it is not." He paused then squinted again. "It is not like now. It is like a mist." He gaped at the translucent version of his mother from last night, perched on the stump, worry imprinted on her face, hands in her smock pocket. More images of her became clear, each image like an imprint seen after looking at the fire too long then glancing away, images one over another until his vision clouded. "Too many."

"Good. Now relax and look again. Concentrate on seeing a few images, not all of them. But do not concentrate too hard. You will eventually be able to go to that time, but that is a skill for another day. It is dangerous until you know how. Very dangerous." She sat again on the log. "See me now and last night. Focus on the times of me here. There will be many."

There were many. Aithagg saw her, the log, the log gone, other logs, other people. It made his head hurt and he shut his eyes from it.

"Relax. It can be overwhelming at first. Focus on me now. Here in time with you." She folder her hands in front of her. Short, haggard fingernails hinted at her worries.

Aithagg focused on her fingernails. He knew his mother worried and why. It was a subject no one spoke of. He had heard his parents speaking in hushed tones about the other siblings that did not survive the ritual. Aithagg resolved to make his mother proud. The ragged fingernails became the only thing visible. The misty versions of his mother and all times past receded until they were barely noticeable.

"I see you, now," he whispered. Then he relaxed his eyes. His mind opened, like releasing a muscle which had been tensed for too long. The misty versions came back, but not overpoweringly. They were there and not there, he saw through them to those short, bitten fingernails. "I see you, then."

"Good. Do not focus too much on the *thens*. Keep them misty," Kei-tha warned. "Because you have not unsynced with time yet—it is a little more difficult. Your body will naturally want to sync into linear time. After you are older and go through the ritual, it will inverse. You will naturally want to be unlocked with time and have to concentrate to sync in." She chuckled then said,

"Eventually, time will be an abstract concept. Something beyond us."

Aithagg barely heard her; he was busy dialing time in and out of his vision. She was there, now. She was there last night. She had been there many times. He looked up and around the circle, mesmerized at the throngs of past misty visions of the tribe which had been here.

"How long have we been coming to the circle?" Aithagg sauntered—looking at the faces and then came to his own. There he stopped for a moment, tilting his head to the side in wonder.

Aithagg looked at his own face, younger than he was now, smiling and laughing with his father. He focused for a moment so the other crowds of misty visions receded and he saw only himself.

His mother's voice came to him from a distance. "We have been here at this circle for 10,000 winters watching the young ones grow and go off into the world. Pushed by the ritual, they go off to claim their place in time. That time is only theirs. It is no more than a blink, the time they lock into." Her voice was quiet, wistful. "We usually do not visit each other there. We stay in solitude."

"Unless your promised one syncs with you to that time?" Aithagg queried.

"Yes."

"Like you and father?"

"Yes."

Aithagg found other misty versions of his parents with other children, hundreds of children through the ages. He looked at the ground to clear his vision. The ground itself was here and now, then and different. The immenseness of time was overwhelming and his head swam.

A hand touched his shoulder and Aithagg looked up into his mother's blue eyes. "How far back did you see?" she asked kindly.

"You had hundreds of children over the ages?" Aithagg asked, his voice a soft whisper.

"I and your father have helped raise 152 young ones since coming to this circle, yes." Kei-tha smoothed his wild curls with an expert touch. "You are seeing much further than most at this age. That is good."

"How far will I be able to see?" He held her hand briefly then let it go.

"Until there was darkness, if you concentrate hard enough," she answered.

He hesitated as if wanting to ask something.

She pulled him in tightly and wrapped her arms around him. She answered the unasked question, "Five." Hoarseness strangled her voice. "Five did not survive the ritual." She smoothed a curl on his head. "Of those that survived, one is near lost to the madness."

"You can see them here," Aithagg stated. It was not a question. He scoured the misty visions of times past around the fire and sought his lost siblings and their curly locks.

"For all of eternity." She hugged him tighter.

"Can you not go back to their time and tell them?" He looked up. "Change it?"

"That is not the way." Her answer was curt but not stern.

"But," he protested.

"We must protect time and not adjust it to our own needs. Else we are no better than the Manipulators we work to save time from." She hugged him even tighter, almost painfully, then let go.

Aithagg looked again at the circle and let the misty images of the past come into view. "Can we see forward?" he asked.

"We can see as far as where time is still unfolding, about 26,000 winters from now. Main-time. The winters are shorter and milder then. The land changes, wildlife changes." Her voice trailed off as if distracted. She continued, "but we can not see past that. Only Eterili can see into the untold future."

Relentlessly he asked, "But we can change things. We can."

"Eterili will have your teeth, willful child. Yes, you can change things in time. It is a fool's path." She took his hand and led him from the circle. "It hurts, a horrible pain when time is manipulated. It is not something you will want to do. It is not."

He interrupted her, "It is not the way." His shoulders slumped slightly. As they left the circle, Aithagg turned once more to look at the past ghosts of children taking their oaths; their parents watching on. He wondered which of those ghosts had been his siblings who did not survive.

Daring to broach a taboo subject, he gently asked, "If I survive, will I go mad like Icaeph?"

"Your brother?" Kei-tha said mostly to herself as she turned to look at her children gathered around the fire in the past: misty memories that would never fade.

Her eyes lingered for a moment near the fire pit. Aithagg followed her gaze and tried to find the past ghost she looked upon with wistfulness. There were so many times to wade through until Aithagg saw: his mother in the past knelt at the side of the fire, nearly in the same spot repeatedly. Over a hundred times she knelt at the side of a child and pressed something into their hands. They then turned and took their place with the others around the fire, ready to proclaim their allegiance to the Vechey and to protect time. One instance, the youth did not accept the gift from his mother and instead patted her on the shoulder before turning to walk away.

"Is that him? He didn't take the gift from you." Aithagg tried to focus tightly on the memory to see clearly.

His mother's tug disrupted him. She tugged on his hand again and urged, "Do not dwell on it. We live too long to mewl over lost moments. To worry on things that cannot be changed is to invite a thirsty beast into your being. That *is* the way of madness. Come along."

Aithagg tried to protest but stopped short when his mother's eyes glared at him.

She said, "Icaeph was rebellious from the start. He still lives, though barely, on the brink of madness, I am to understand. It hurts me that I should not go to him and he will not return to here to be promised to another, to raise children of his own, to be a part of us." She paused, then patted Aithagg's hand. "We are a people alone, forever, across time. It is a long time and you have to protect yourself from the madness that can creep in." She glanced back to the memories around the fire. "Perhaps it is a blessing more than a curse."

She startled, realizing she had spoken aloud when Aithagg asked perplexed, "The madness?"

Kei-tha looked at Aithagg sharply. "Eterili will have our teeth. Let us dwell no further on things that we can not change lest we court madness ourselves."

# 7 MADNESS

Icaeph
Unnamed

25,000　　　　◄┼┼ Present Day

He lie there in darkness. His mind whirled in circles, pain pulled at his very being. Was it day yet in main-time, the present? Was it night? Was the moon up, the sun? Incoherent as agony filled his core, he sat against the rock wall willing the swirling around him to still. It did not abate.

Icaeph tried to muster the energy to crawl forward. He lacked enough to move his arms. Instead, he slid sideways until his face touched the ground. Turning his head, he lay his cheek against the cold earth. His body drew energy from the ground, greedily. He tried to concentrate on main-time, where the weight of the sun's rays would pull at him. He had forgotten to eat, to take sustenance. His body, lacking enough fuel to move, began to shut down. Icaeph welcomed the thought of an end. He closed his eyes against the darkness. He would rest. Perhaps he would rest a little more and seek food when he awoke.

Pain, an aching, pulsed through his bones, his hair, his eyelids.

At some point his body slowed and relaxed, its pulls of energy from the dirt became deep, rhythmic. Icaeph began to drift into slumber. The moment he inhabited was thousands of winters before main-time. This time is where his body had synchronized to, after he had come of age and went through the ritual. Here is where time froze for him and he came and went as he pleased. This cave he slept in provided a safe place for him and the soil in it and around it provided enough sustenance to keep him alive. He would need to eat to thrive but the energy found in the earth itself—the rock, the dust—would keep him from perishing. He stretched further out on the rock floor and lay his arms and palms on the ground, pulling more energy. He relaxed further and fell asleep.

With sleep, his body disappeared from his frozen-time. It shifted throughout time, appearing 20,000 winters before, in main-time, 60,000 winters before, near his frozen-time and so on. The chamber he slept in had been open for a million years, though the height of the ceiling had shrunk over the millennia. Thus, he shifted through time safely without colliding into solid stone.

Appearing, reappearing, disappearing throughout the ages; unbothered in his dark, earthen tomb.

A noise in the distant brought him to consciousness. Icaeph struggled to find out whether he was in his time, main-time, or some other time. He shook his head to clear it as if shaking off cobwebs. It only made the world spin about him more. The noise registered again to his ears. As if through mounds of furs, a thought came to him. Sound. Hearing sound. Not in frozen-time—sound does not carry there: nothing moves or makes a sound. Synced with time then. Is it now or then? He pondered and searched for the sun's path, which had always been so clear to him. Unable to find the sun, Icaeph's limbs hung numb and thick. Another thought made it through the wet mounds of fur in his head; perhaps he should go find food and his head would clear. He needed to feed.

Icaeph rolled onto his side. Skin scraped across dirt and pebbles. A distant sound again—what was it? He listened intently.

*Click.*
*Tap. Tap.*
*Scrape.*
*Scritch.*
*Scraaaape.*
*Click. Tap. Tap.*

A sound of rock against rock.

*Sccccraape.*
*Click.*
*Clack. Click. Click.*
*Tap. Tap. Tap.*
*Scraaape.*

He oriented his ears towards the sound and began to move closer, making no sound himself. The scraping and clicking continued in long and short bursts punctuated by staccato tapping sounds. Icaeph's weary body, numb and heavy as stone itself, inched forward towards the tapping sound.

When Icaeph smelled the Linear all conscious thought left him.

A short man, wide in stature, stood at the rock wall. He held in his hand a sharpened antler and, in the other hand, a flattened rock. He raised the rock and hit it on the blunt end of the antler. The antler scraped down the rock wall, creating a groove.

*Scrrraaape.*
*Click. Tap. Tap.*

He raised his hand again to strike the antler. Icaeph was upon the man before he struck the blow. A nearby torch, propped in a rock cairn, fell to the side. It cast long shadows of the brutality. Dark blood spattered across the petroglyphs on the wall. The darkness dripped to the dirt floor and dried. Gurgled cries fell silent as Icaeph fed greedily.

Icaeph blinked up at the dark ceiling. He was not sure where he was. Turning he saw the corpse; gaping maw where the throat had been, eyes wide with surprise and terror, coagulated blood pooled in the dirt beneath it.

Icaeph's wide mouth tightened into a frown. Apparently, he had fed. Though he did not remember it. Wisps of memories gained from the Linear whirled in Icaeph's brain: the hunt the night before, celebration, feasting, mating. Icaeph grimaced again trying to shake the Linear's experiences from his mind. He loathed the sweat and feces smell coming from the corpse and imagined the foreign memories in his head smelled of rot. Rotten, foul smelling memories would float in his brain until dissipated.

He blinked at the dark ceiling again. What time was he in? The sun was out. Main-time. Icaeph closed his eyes. The Linear's blood had helped restore some of his energy—enough to find where he was in time. He dared not fall asleep in this area of the cave. It was a recent passage that had opened with passaging water over the thousands of years but was solid rock in the past. If Icaeph fell asleep here, he would more than likely become embedded in solid rock 20,000 winters ago. Would he cease to exist? Though death had seemed inviting not but a moment ago, sobered, he did not yearn for destruction. Not as much.

Icaeph still did not have the energy to stand. He crawled on hands and knees until he found his safe chamber farther back in the cave. He wondered, before falling asleep, if the Linears would travel back this far? He did not think so. Their torches of fire would extinguish before they reached his chamber. His last thought was of the rotting corpse. He would have to dispose of that soon. Sleep overtook him. Once again, he disappeared.

It was night in main-time when he awoke. He was sure of it. Icaeph stood, weakly, and listened. No sound. Nothing moved. He was safe in his frozen moment of time where only he existed.

Slowly, unsteady on his feet, Icaeph shuffled soundlessly through the cave passage. The pebbles and dirt stirred by his feet moved and scattered through time, landed minutes forward and behind his time. He stooped and crawled through passages too low for him to walk in. He slid in and out of time to when the passages were wider, careful to not collide with himself when he had previously slid through time there, then returned to his frozen-time where a collision was not a concern. Shortly he approached the corpse in main-time. Icaeph looked. The ghostly images of the Linear entering the cave and drawing were clear and stark in the darkness. Icaeph tried not to focus on the equally clear and stark images of when he had crawled like a rodent towards the Linear—ripped the throat out, then lapped at the fount. The ghostly image of himself crawling away became focused. Icaeph unconsciously moved out of the way so he did not touch the loathsome ghost version of himself crawling in the dirt, mad with hunger. Icaeph looked down at his body, covered in blood and dirt. When in his frozen-time, dirt would not stick or react with him. However, in Linear-time he had literally rolled in the blood-mixed mud and stank nearly as much as the corpse. Icaeph wrinkled his nose in disgust as he synced into main-time. His smell and the smell of the corpse were a physical presence.

He grabbed the body of the dead Linear and gathered it to him. The tongue, purple and swollen, poked from the mouth. The eyes, wide and unseeing, covered with sand and grit, lolled at him. Even weak as he was, the body weighed less than a bundle of twigs to Icaeph. He carried the Linear towards the entrance of the cave. This closest entrance was small. Icaeph had to place the body on the ground and crawl out, pulling the body after him by its moccasin clad foot. Being in main-time, the sound of the dragging was loud and obnoxious. Icaeph stood and gathered the corpse again. He slipped into a time so long ago ice covered the ground and the entrance to his cave was too small for a mouse to enter. Here he walked south until he came to a depression in the ground. Water bubbled up in a sulfur spring. Steam rose from it. He threw the body into the small water outlet where it sank, mostly. The dark water covered the corpse greedily. Icaeph watched it sink. A solitary limb floated at the top. It too would eventually sink. Icaeph turned his back and returned to his frozen-time.

He would clean the stink from himself and go feed. Movement at the edge of his vision caught his eye.

Nothing can move in his frozen-time except for him. What was moving? He darted his head from side to side to find the cause.

There was nothing.

Icaeph paused and puzzled at the trees and grass, frozen in mid breeze, where he had seen something.

Imagining things? He wondered.

A wave of dizziness crashed over him. He would need to feed soon. He must have gone for winters without eating. The one Linear was enough to bring him back to reality but not sustain him for long. Thankfully, the rotten taste of the Linear's memories were already fading.

Icaeph reached forward to main-time looking for the close-by encampment. A force like a warm and heavy lead ball rolled in the front of his brain until it stopped—pointing towards where the Linears were. They were a small tribe. He had fed on them for hundreds of winters. One weary foot at a time, Icaeph walked towards their camp.

A singular small fire was still burning. The Linears were mostly asleep. A lone watchman stood at the edge of the camp facing the river. The ghost images of these Linears stretched in front of Icaeph as he looked on from his frozen moment thousands of years in the past. He walked through the camp focusing on main-time, ignoring all the previous nights he had been here, and searched for the Linear who would serve him best tonight.

The elder of the group slept on a palette of hides elevated at the head by bundles of thatched leaves. His breathing labored, and he shook with the effort of it. Icaeph slipped into main-time and knelt by the aged Linear. He bent and with control, drank deeply from the Linear, drawing energy from his skin and blood from the pulse in his neck. Icaeph grimaced as the memories and fragmented thoughts invaded him as he drank. The Linear smelled of curdled milk. The touch of the leathery skin sent energy through Icaeph and made the fine hairs on the back of his arms stand on end. He pulled away and sat still for a moment, the energy flowed through him. Roughly, he touched the wounds at the Linear's neck and they began to heal. The Linear snored a deep, loud inhale once then began to breathe evenly again.

Icaeph wiped his mouth with the back of his hand and sneered. Killing them all would give no satisfaction. Nor would he have food when he next hungered. He loathed the need to feed upon these Linears. Hated them. Hated himself. Hated time.

Movement flickered again at the edge of his vision. Icaeph worried the watchman had spotted him. Quickly, Icaeph slipped back into his frozen-time in the past, safely away from any observers.

There were none.

In the night's safety, Icaeph began to walk through the woods and unconsciously synced with main-time again. He did not even realize he had synced until the first raindrops fell upon his skin. Careless. Even in the woods, in the dead of night, Linears might have seen him. To a Linear he would have appeared out of thin air, a cold gust of wind to mark his appearance. The rain fell more steadily. His filthy clothes began to stick to his skin. He raised his long, oval face to the clouds and welcomed the cool wetness. Nearby a fawn stepped away from the tree line and paused. Icaeph did not notice. Neither did he notice the lone man who knelt in the shadows of the trees, downwind.

Rivulets of blood and dirt ran down Icaeph's face, cleansed by the rain. He raised his hands to wipe his eyes dry. Another movement caught his attention, then he heard the hiding man's heartbeat. Icaeph wiped his eyes dry again and peered into the dark woods. The heat of the man and the ghost images of his progress through the woods became clear to Icaeph. He considered syncing back to his frozen-time but hesitated. He knew this Linear not by sight but by attitude.

"Manipulator." He gave a slight bow then smiled. "You have been quiet for a while."

The lone man stood and came forward from the trees, but did not dare come too close. His voice cracked when he answered as if unused for some time, "It took some time to find this host. No thanks to you."

"I thought you might enjoy a cave salamander as a host for a change. Linears must get boring." Icaeph came closer to the man.

The man took a step backwards.

Icaeph repeated himself unsure if he had said his thought aloud already or not, "A cave salamander. Thought you would enjoy a break from Line…" His voice trailed off in mid-thought.

The man took a step towards Icaeph. He appeared severely disheveled with half of his waistcloth in tatters, dried blood on his chest and thighs. A necklace of finger bones clattered around his neck. He held out a hand. "You yourself have been silent too. I have not seen you for a hundred winters or more."

Icaeph looked at him questioningly.

"You have lost track have you not?" The Manipulator tilted his chin towards Icaeph. "Losing your grasp." An evil grin, a predator's smile, appeared on his face. He took another step closer.

Icaeph did not move. He stared at the Manipulator.

The man took another tentative step closer. The nearby fawn darted back into the woods for safety. Neither paid attention to the noise the fawn made crashing through the thicket.

The Manipulator grinned wider and chided, "It would be most delicious—" He stepped closer, holding his hands close to his sides. "—if I had you as a host. Imagine how quickly I would destroy the universe and be released from this never-ending hell."

In a rush, the Manipulator jumped at Icaeph, raising high a dagger made of stone.

Icaeph stepped sideways without hesitation and the Manipulator plunged to the ground. He rolled and grunted.

"I can see your decisions before you make them, like ghosts in the air." Icaeph spat on the ground. "You are tiresome."

With that Icaeph slipped away into his frozen-time. He saw the Manipulator, now as a ghost image in main-time, prone on the dirt. He did not hear the scream of frustration erupting from the Manipulator, framed with a wide-open mouth, bulging eyes, hands clenched in fists.

"He probably woke the tribe," Icaeph surmised.

Turning his back, Icaeph walked towards his home and thought of his Manipulator no more that night.

\*\*\*

Icaeph rested in the darkness deep inside the cave, his cave, which he had called home since his youth. Here the light of the sun had never existed at any time. The complete darkness was a respite.

He tried to remember his youth before the ritual, before becoming locked here in this place where time stopped for all but him. Trapped. Memories tried to surface, elusive, vague. They faded from his grasp.

The sun rose in main-time. Having eaten and gained some strength he would be able to stay active in his frozen-times for at least two winters or more. He sat, unable not muster the desire to stir. Outside, the Manipulator changed and adjusted time.

Slight changes. Moving things here.

The season faded, the next season mellowed the cold.

Adjusting things there.

Another season faded and the air outside warmed.

Killing. Baiting one tribe to attack another. Each adjustment caused the river of time to hiccup in its tracks and adjust. One by one, the adjustments compounded, and the universe listed slightly.

Icaeph ached with each molestation of time and weakened as the seasons passed. Yet, he lay still in the dark and ignored the world. Let it collapse. Let the Linears die. Let their stinking, dirt covered bodies rot like so many corpses; bloated, with tongues lolling.

Cave crickets crawled across his face. He did not move. Their feet, delicate and ephemeral as his memories, touched his cold skin. He brushed at the cave crickets that had crawled onto his eyelids.

Bright lights blinked at the side of his vision like fireflies. He turned his head slowly to see. Only darkness.

He knew. There was no mistaking. This must be what madness looks like as it creeps in. What did it matter?

Absently, he realized he must have slipped into time again; else there would be no cave crickets. Yes, this must be madness. A forgetfulness and disintegration. He slipped back to his frozen-time. The cave crickets that had been on his eyelids came with him. Stunned by the transition, they froze and fell off his face.

He looked at them, able to see in the darkness with clarity, and wondered if they were dead. He watched. They did not move.

Dead.

He envied them.

*\*\*\**

The moon was full, the winter harsh, when he next exited his sanctum. He stood, naked in the moonlight, synced with main-time. Blinking, he looked at the stars. He did not remember what he had done with his clothing, when he had last eaten, why he was standing here. Icaeph tried to muster some emotion; embarrassment, anger, hate—anything to feel.

Nothing.

He searched mentally for the Manipulator and found their disruptions. These disruptions caused the time streams to pull from their course and burned like shattered bone shards in his veins. Icaeph needed to fix these things; he had sworn to keep time safe from the Manipulator. He would fix them. He always had. For how many winters?

Icaeph paused, thinking to himself, unable to remember. It must have been many, many winters. He began walking again, slipping between his frozen-time, main-time and other random times. He was nearly unobserved, a naked specter visible to only the wildlife for only a second before he disappeared again into another time. Eventually, he realized he was approaching a molested moment. In his vision, the white ghosts of the Linears began to appear. It was the nearby tribe he usually fed upon. Icaeph was in his frozen-time again, luckily, and unobserved. The elder lay on his elevated bed with a spear protruding from his chest. The elder's mouth gaped in a horrible slack-jawed grimace of death. The ghostly image of the spear and elder, however, were not white as normal images of time were to Icaeph. Instead, they were a ghastly yellow, tinged and tainted with a putrefied ocher.

These things were not of the normal timeline. The Manipulator had created this mayhem. It would throw the time stream off track. The early death of the elder might spark some controversy. The details of it did not matter to Icaeph. Perhaps the spear was from another tribe and the death would cause a battle between the tribes: more than likely. Icaeph did not care; it only mattered this should not exist in this time. It needed fixing.

The gasps of the Linears caused Icaeph to look up from the elder. He had slipped into main-time and stood, stark naked, near the elder. Quickly he synced back to his frozen-time. Icaeph held out his hand for balance. He had to get a hold of himself.

Looking back through time, Icaeph saw where the Manipulator, intent on killing the elder, visited the camp in the night. Icaeph considered stepping in and killing the Manipulator before he harmed the elder. The difficulty was once killed—the Manipulator would inhabit the closest thing to him. It was best to drag him off and make sure the thing to inhabit was some cave cricket, salamander, or something equally limited in range. He had to make sure he was not touching or close to the Manipulator when he killed him, lest he be the host. It would be a living death even worse than his trapped existence now. Icaeph considered his options carefully.

His vision swam, and the pain deepened in his bones as time shifted even further. Icaeph quickly turned and went back to where he had encountered the Manipulator in the woods those seasons ago.

Icaeph, from his vantage point, saw a clothed version of himself standing in the clearing looking up at the rain as it fell upon his face. The Manipulator approached carefully, step by step. Icaeph with tattered clothing dripping wet, stood there slightly confused. A fawn grazed nearby.

Icaeph did not remember what they had said. The Manipulator took his first menacing step forward dedicated on killing the immobile Icaeph.

Icaeph focused on that time and stepped into it. He forgot any confusion or weakness. His only purpose now was to kill the Manipulator, ending his ability to thrust a spear through the Linear chief's chest in the future.

He stepped into the time. Both the Manipulator and the other, confused version of himself, turned towards Icaeph, who stood before them naked and seething. Icaeph grabbed the Manipulator and pushed him towards the fawn. Both were upon the fawn before it registered the bipeds' appearance. The confused, clothed Icaeph only stood gaping in the rain, his brain lost and still muddled.

The Manipulator had only the hosts' strength, the strength of a Linear. However, lacking fear of pain or mortality enabled him to fight more ferociously than a mere Linear might. He spun and struck at Icaeph with his dagger.

Icaeph was unsurprised by the attack and ducked it effortlessly, as he usually did. Instead, he grabbed the dagger and plunged it into the neck of the Manipulator and pinned him to a tree.

He grabbed the fawn before it could dart away and placed it at the feet of the writhing and kicking Manipulator. He hobbled it with a nearby vine.

He watched the Manipulator writhe. The fawn now at his feet. Kick. Still. Kick. Kick. Still. For a moment nothing moved save the blood dripping from the gaping wound in the Manipulator's neck. Suddenly, the fawn startled: eyes flew wide open, its breath came in huge gasps. Then it began to spasm and writhe on the ground, feet sporadically kicking and bucking. Dirt flew in chunks and landed on the dead host's feet, which dangled inches off of the forest floor.

Icaeph turned his back and slipped away through time. He had seen the possession process a thousand times before. In front of him was the original Icaeph, ghostly white and translucent, still confused and looking at the rain. Icaeph watched himself, turn and amble back towards the cave. The embarrassment he had searched for earlier hit him squarely in the chest as hard as a fist. He was becoming a doddering old fool, the shame of it. The ghostly version of himself disappeared as it had slipped into the frozen-time where there were no ghost versions of himself. Icaeph slumped. An old fool. What had Eterili said about the madness? Could he stave it off somehow?

# 8 LAST ONE THERE

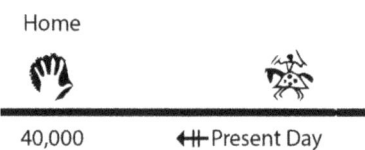

"One. Two. Three," he hid his eyes and counted. Around him he heard the others giggling and running. The air moved as they slid into time and hid from one another. He heard them disappear. The air closed into the space they had once occupied.

*Pop.*

*Pop.*

*Pop.*

Aithagg was older, nearly twelve, and had become accustomed to seeing time unfold as ghosts without becoming overwhelmed. He kept his eyes hidden and continued to count, "Four. Five. Six. Seven."

"No peeking!" Catha squeaked from nearby before she slipped away through time and the air closed in with a pop.

Aithagg continued to count, patiently, "Fourteen. Fifteen." He turned and looked around the woods then called, "Beware!"

At first he saw nothing, the ghost images did not readily appear unless he thought about them. He concentrated looking for Otski, Ygolz or Catha. Then he saw the ghost trails of where they had gone. Slowly, at first too transparent to differentiate from one another, they began to appear. Then he saw them. Otski had climbed up a tree and was hiding about a winter ago. The tree had lost its leaves. Ygolz had stood directly in the open, but cleverly was in the same spot he had occupied yesterday so his ghosts overlapped. Catha was nowhere or when to be seen.

Aithagg slipped into the time where Ygolz stood and tagged him gently on the shoulder. "TAG!" he shouted.

The two slipped back to home-time together, giggling.

"I was in the same place. How did you see me?" Ygolz asked. He placed the palm of his hand at the base of his nose and pushed up while sniffling. A white crease sat just above the end of his nose from the repeated pushing at his nose.

"Easy. It looked darker, the ghost images. Good try though!" Aithagg turned and looked towards Otski, whose ghost was visible a hundred winters ago. "Look at Otski." He nudged Ygolz with an elbow. "He will get cold soon and come down. Should I just leave him there?"

Ygolz squinted, held his hands up to cover his eyes as if they were in daylight and squinted more. "He's too stubborn to come down. He'll stay there thinking you can't see back that far until he turns to ice."

Aithagg considered and then nodded. "You are right." He disappeared.

Ygolz tried to squint to see Aithagg as he tagged Otski back a hundred winters ago but already he was losing his focus on that time. He was unable see back that far.

A gush of cold air pushed at him as both Aithagg and Otski appeared in front of him.

Otski had his arms crossed and was objecting, "That is not fair. How can you see back that far?"

Aithagg laughed. "If you can not see back that far, how could you go there? You might have collided with something!"

Otski turned his back to Aithagg, his arms still crossed. "I can so."

Aithagg looked back towards the tree and the smiled. "Oh. I see. You took multiple steps. Went as far as you could see. Stopped. Then went as far as you could see back from there. I get it." He turned towards Otski. "That is clever. Multiple steps."

Flattered, Otski uncrossed his arms and faced Aithagg and Ygolz. "That is a pretty good idea, right?" he beamed.

The boys congratulated each other on their cleverness while Aithagg continued to look around for Catha.

He turned and looked, searching as far back as his vision would allow. He looked back to before they had approached this area of the woods and picked a spot in time where no one had been. He slipped there. From this vantage point he saw forward in time to when the four had walked here from the circle and began to disappear one by one. He watched as he had gone to a nearby gnarled tree, covered his eyes and began counting. This was cheating, standing back in time and watching. The game was to flex and train their vision of time. Was this not flexing and training his vision of time?

Catha had stood, would stand, near him as he hid his eyes and began counting. Aithagg watched the ghost images of the Catha. She stood there and watched Aithagg counting then turned and quietly walked away. She snuck away, her braided hair bouncing with each step. She had turned and said something then slipped out of time. However, she only slipped back in time by a small amount.

He watched as Catha appeared back in time just about where he had been at "ten" in his counting. She walked calmly away and hid behind the same tree he was hiding his eyes on. Since she was in the time with Aithagg, he did not think to look at the same time he was occupying. He looked in the past, naturally, and missed her.

"Very clever," he whispered.

He crept behind the tree and leaned against it, not looking to see where his other self was. He focused on the Catha and slid into time with her at just the moment his other self finished counting and exclaimed, "Beware!"

Both Aithaggs had their hands on the tree in almost the same position.

"Tag," Aithagg whispered in her ear.

Catha pointed at Aithagg's hand and gasped, "You almost collided with yourself!" She turned to him in horror.

He looked at his hand on the tree trunk then at where his other self's hand had been. His other self had already turned and disappeared into time. Aithagg calmly and cavalierly shook off the near miss. "I saw it," he lied.

"Did not," she countered.

"I did. And you are very tricky." Aithagg stood and tried not to look at where he had almost collided with himself. Had he slipped into time and occupied a space that was already occupied, whether it was himself or someone else—he would have obliterated what was there. The last one to appear occupies the space. He wondered, absently, if it would have hurt. Excruciatingly, he surmised.

Both returned to where Otski and Ygolz stood.

"Found her," Aithagg called.

Catha did not mention the error which might have cost him a finger. Aithagg looked at her appreciatively. She lowered her eyes and only smiled. Otski and Ygolz missed the exchange of looks.

"I am hungry. Do you want to go see if there is any bread left?" Ygolz asked of Otski. He raised his arm and swiped at his nose. "Last one there!" He pushed at Ygolz and then ran off.

Otski ran after him leaving Aithagg and Catha standing alone.

"Thank you," Aithagg stated simply, but with tenderness.

"You do not make fun of me for not seeing very far back in time. It is the least I could do. Thank you," she said in return. She grabbed his hand and squeezed it gently then let go.

Awkwardly, they turned together and headed back towards the circle. Aithagg hesitated then pushed at her shoulder and shouted, "Last one there!"

He ran.

She giggled and ran after him.

\*\*\*

The boys had already joined the others in the great room of the cave. Torches were lit; smoke staining the rock ceiling with its soot. The adults saw well enough in the darkness without the torches. The youths were still developing not only their sight for seeing through time but also for seeing in the dark. The flickering light cast lanky shadows along the walls and floors.

Aithagg was the last to arrive. The group stood in clusters, murmuring to one another. He met his father's searching eyes. They nodded to one another as Aithagg approached.

"We should go soon and make sure you eat. You are growing and need to eat daily." His father held up a hand when Aithagg started to protest. "*Daily*. Even if you do not feel like it. When you are grown you can go winters without eating. Not yet, though."

His mother approached. "Did you wash?" She checked his hands and looked him over from top to bottom. "They will smell you if you do not wash."

Aithagg held out his hands for inspection like a small child. "Mother," he protested gently.

She ignored the protests, looked, and proclaimed him clean, "Be careful."

Fathers and sons, daughters and mothers, paired off and left the cave.

Once outside the pairs wandered in different directions, then disappeared as some slipped into main-time.

Aithagg and his father walked down a small path to a stream. It babbled peacefully. Aithagg looked at the water wearingly.

"Look to see where the water isn't here or isn't as deep. It makes it easier to cross." Iskeho slipped into time where the stream had nearly dried from a drought. He crossed the streambed. Aithagg followed.

Once done, they both slipped back to their normal home-time.

"Why does it hurt so much to walk in water?" Aithagg asked.

"I would guess it is because it separates us more from the earth where we gather strength," Iskeho answered. "When Eterili called to us and we crossed the islands in boats—it was very painful. Unbearable to some. It was a long journey. We carried dirt from our homeland in the hulls of our boats. It helped but did not eliminate the discomfort." He snorted. "I never want to be on the open water again."

"Why did she come here?" Aithagg stumbled over a rock, his adolescence ungainliness getting the best of him, and caught himself before falling.

"She says the rocks called to her. She followed their call until she found this cave which is large enough to hold all of our people from all of time at once, if needed." Iskeho reached out and steadied Aithagg with a hand.

They walked for a while in silence, following the stream. Eventually they came upon a small camp. The people there had shored their boats and were asleep in various positions about the bank; some inside of tents made of rawhide; others under lean-tos made of branches.

Iskeho held his hand out to silence the boy. "You have to feed while synced in main-time," he said. "If you try to feed in a time that has gone by it can sustain you, but not for long. The blood of the Linear is what keeps them tied to time. You have to feed in the time of *now* not *then*." Iskeho looked at him. "Does that make sense?"

Aithagg shook his head.

"See how this is now. There is no time after this, yet. This is main-time. The Linears live and move with this now-time." Iskeho held his hand up. "Now look back and see the older moments, the ghost images you see. That is then. Or before, if you prefer. It is not the current main-time. If you slip into that passed time and try to feed, the blood will not keep you filled for very long. You have to feed on blood in the main-time."

Aithagg looked at him, slightly puzzled.

Iskeho shrugged. "Somehow the blood is connected to time. It is how they sync. We do not sync, but need it to survive." He smiled. "I know what works and what does not work, not necessarily why."

Aithagg frowned. "What if you go to a then-time and change something and the path of time goes a different way?"

"The amount of time that has passed does not change." Iskeho scanned the sleeping group to make sure none stirred. "Like the river that changes its course, the water is still the same amount—it has moved its direction. And no matter the other timelines generated we are moored to this one."

They crept closer and Iskeho indicated with a hand Aithagg should feed. Iskeho would supervise. He saw a ghostly white figure of a Linear in main-time.

Aithagg stilled and concentrated while Iskeho watched. The young boy hesitated and looked at his father.

"The now is not where our home-time is?" Aithagg queried.

"The now is many winters ahead of where our home-time is," his father answered.

"Why?" The boy paused and tilted his head to the side.

"Home-time is the time where we all sync to in unison when it is time to raise a family. When you go through the ritual, you will then sync to your own personal-time. A mere second of time.

There is a time for each: our home, your home," Iskeho patiently answered. "Home-time is where we can co-exist outside of time and from there exist in a Linear fashion. Your time will be a special moment outside of time as well just for you."

"Why?"

"It is the way."

"Do we choose our time, the one after the ritual?"

"It chooses us, I believe."

Aithagg tilted his head again and was about to continue his questioning.

"You are stalling. Do not fool me. Time to show me you can feed." Iskeho crossed his arms and looked at the boy sternly. "Take care to not wake them. Again."

The boy blushed slightly at the memory, then set his shoulders straight and looked again at the reclined figures. He tensed as he concentrated, then wavered slightly as he disappeared.

Iskeho saw the ghost image of the boy as he entered main-time with the sleeping Linears. Iskeho watched from home-time and let the boy occupy the space alone.

Aithagg looked back towards his father, who appeared as a ghost image in the past, yet stood only 3 feet from him. He smiled at the figure with its arms crossed, then turned to his task. Around him lay two snoring figures. He glanced around to make sure no one was awake or stirring. None were. He knelt to the closest sleeping figure. For the moment he became lost in the breathing of the Linear: rhythmic, deep. The barrel chest of the Linear expanded with the breath and then deflated. The snoring reached his ears, and he marveled at the baritone. Knowing his father might become impatient or concerned for discovery, Aithagg tore himself from the study of breathing.

He, himself, did not breathe—nor did any of his kind. They had the capability but not the need. Breath was only drawn to speak with. When he was younger, he and his friends would pretend to breathe as they played at being Linears and made games of pretending to feed upon one another.

Aithagg leaned towards the sleeping figure and laid his fangs to the large neck. He took care to apply only so much pressure and not too much. It would do no good to leave blood trails and cause alarm when the Linear awoke in the morning. He had practiced many times to keep control. Aithagg allowed himself a breath in order to smell the warm, metallic blood. It electrified him at once and he became engrossed all the more in the volume of blood as it spray into his mouth and course through his being. He drank deeply. Memories from the Linear filled his brain and tingled his nerves. Things he had no knowledge of became his own experiences, then faded like a dream.

Aware of his father's watching eyes, Aithagg carefully touched his tongue to the Linear's wounds. They healed nearly instantly. He sat back on his heels and looked at the Linear, surveying the results of his feed. The wounds on the neck had become reduced to small pink spots. The spots would disappear by morning. The Linear snored on as if nothing had occurred. Not a drop had spilled.

Pleased with himself Aithagg stood and looked back through time to find his father. He then slid into that time returning somewhere close to when he had left.

To his father, Aithagg had disappeared for only a minute before he returned. Both watched into the future where Aithagg would feed.

After a moment of silence, Iskeho turned and said, "Well done."

They spoke not another word as they walked back towards the cave where the others would be waiting. Aithagg glowed with the vigor of a Vechey newly fed. Though the adults survived 40 winters on one solid feeding, the youth needed to feed weekly at a minimum while they grew to maintain their health. Wisps of memories from the Linear swirled in Aithagg's mind as he walked, starry-eyed, by his father's side. Many memories were not age-appropriate, no matter the species. He glanced at his father, guiltily, knowing his father had no way of knowing the memories flooding his senses. The warm guilt of them flushed his cheeks.

The moon lay on the horizon; a bloated, glowing toad. Around the youngsters the night animals creaked, croaked, and otherwise made a racket. In the distance, a large animal sounded its trumpeting call. Otski tried to answer.

"That's not how it sounds," Ygolz critiqued, then tried to do his own imitation of the big-toothed creature grunting loudly trying to attract mates.

Aithagg and Catha consorted in murmurs then announced in unison, "Ygolz is the winner."

Ethasa, who had stood at the fire pit among the other teens preparing for their ritual, sat apart from the others. Unusually quiet, he looked across the moonlit valley silently.

The other three eventually nudged each other to get their attention and pointed towards Ethasa. Eyebrows rose. Fingers pointed. Shoulders shrugged.

Silence settled across all three until they were as still as Ethasa.

They watched as the bloated toad of a moon sunk slowly until it was out of sight.

No one spoke. The silence stretched out between them.

The first glimmer of light threatened on the opposite horizon, eclipsed by a rock-face. The birth of the sun burned as if it were a hot, brisk wind on their faces. Ethasa would have to leave soon. Being older and able to see further back in time, he was unable to stand even the barest of sunlight. When the sun rose, he would experience all energy of sunlight that had ever existed in the time visible to him. It was too much to bear.

The younger children, with limited sight through time, would experience a limited buildup of the sun permitting them to stay in the daylight for a few moments more. Most elders would suffer near intolerable pain if they stayed in the daylight.

The game was to stay out in the sunlight as long as it was tolerable. Each one daring the others to stay as long as possible before the pain became unbearable.

Though Aithagg was younger, he saw more of time than most; however, he tolerated the sun a little more than the others.

The sun crept a little closer towards dawn and the surrounding night began to abate.

Ethasa began to squirm and rub at his arms. Ygolz and Otski fidgeted. Aithagg and Catha sat still.

The first rays of sunlight broke across the horizon. Somewhere a parent called, "Time to come in."

No one moved a muscle.

Red blood sweat beaded on Ethasa's forehead. Impatiently he wiped it from his eyes. A few more moments passed and he jumped up as if poked with a stick on fire.

"Eterili," he cursed and stomped back towards the cave, slipping into a darker time in the past to calm the pain from the sun.

Ygolz and Otski nudged each other in the ribs as they taunted.

"You go."

"You go."

"You first."

"You first."

They stared at each other; pink blood sweat beading on their forehead and cheeks. Otski blinked the stinging out of his eyes.

Ygolz jumped up and pushed at Otski shouting, "Last one there." He ran off, back into time, into darkness, towards the cave.

Otski had not even stood up before he disappeared back into time. Aithagg and Catha watched the ghost images as the two boys ran through the night back towards the cave.

Aithagg turned to the girl. "It does not bother you does it?"

She looked at her hands and did not answer.

Sweat, bright red, had broken out on his face and dripped down his sharp nose.

"It is not the winner that can stay the longest. It is the loser," she whispered. "It is the one who can not feel the sun." Large wide-eyes filled with sorrow turned to Aithagg. "Please do not tell anyone," she pleaded.

"I will not," Aithagg promised.

"I can not see into time. I am not bothered by the sun." Catha touched the dirt beside her. "I can not feel the earth call to me."

"You will. It just takes a little longer sometimes," Aithagg explained.

She cut him off with a small raised hand.

He silenced.

They sat a moment longer. Aithagg tried to not fidget, though the pain was crawling through his body as steadily as the sun was rising.

Catha turned to him and reached up to wipe the sweat from his forehead. He allowed it, not daring to look into her eyes.

"Let us go." She took his hand and led him towards the cave.

They climbed up over rocks to a wide entrance, deep set into the hillside. The air was crisp and cool as the sun began to brighten the sky's dark black with its pale warmth.

Catha held his hand for a moment more as she paused at the entrance to watch the sunrise. Aithagg was desperately trying to hide the physical pain the sun was causing him. Pink patches spread on his loose clothing around his armpits, neck, and the small of his back. He held on to her hand and endured to wait. Eventually, he squeezed her hand and let go, having to retreat further into the darkness of the cave.

"I have to," he apologized. "I'm sorry." His voice, a mournful whisper.

She smiled and said, "I used to sneak out and watch the sun rise. Still do."

Aithagg looked behind him in the darkness. He had retreated past the incoming light. He worried, "Voices carry in here. Please. Be careful."

As if to make the point clear, the wind from the entrance rushed past her in a gust and caused her dark hair to obscure her face. She reached up with a trembling hand and pulled it away, then wiped away tears quickly, tilting her head down to hide the movement.

Aithagg stepped forward, trying to get closer. The sun's rays, even in this twilight, kept him back. All of light in all of time is too much energy for a Vechey to endure. The dim light lit the tops of the rocks on the floor at the entrance. Catha's shadow rippled across the rocks like a translucent, shadowy stream. The sun began to highlight the bridge of her nose and eyes, the wet patches under her eyes and on her cheeks glistened. He stopped, unable to come closer. Instead, he offered his hand, avoiding the incoming rays of the sun.

"Do you think you'll go? Leave? Before the ritual." His hand stayed outreached.

She turned, scratching sounds as her feet kicked up pebbles and grit gave a backdrop to her words. "I should." She stepped forward and joined Aithagg in the darkness, taking his hand.

Together they walked further into the darkness, slowly, letting their eyes adjust.

"There is time," she said more to herself than Aithagg.

\*\*\*

At the fire ring, on the other side of the hill from Aithagg and Catha, Eterili spoke with a group of small children.

"Time is a circle, but you will never know it." Eterili sat on a rock near the fire. The children gathered around to hear her stories, a rare treat. They did not gather too closely, for it had been at least a millennium since she had bathed. "An ant walking on the mountain does not see the shape of the mountain."

A distant wolf howled and Eterili raised her head as if to listen then continued her story. She held a gnarled stick in one hand and drew in the dirt. The nearby fire flickered dancing shadows across her illustrations.

She drew a line in the sand.

"This is time. Here at the end, on the leading edge of time are the Linears. We call that edge main-time. Linears live in main-time day after day and cannot leave it. Trapped. Fortunate for them they live short lives."

The children, her rapt pupils not daring enough to interrupt the ancient Eterili, listened intently.

She drew another line to the left of the first.

"This is time long ago from where the edge of time is," she said.

A brave youngster interjected, "The edge of time is where the Linears live. Main-time. Where we'll feed when we are older." He looked around proudly.

"Yes, yes. Where you feed," she answered, then pointed with her stick to the line drawn on the left. "We are here 40,000 winters or so behind main-time. It is a safe time where Linears will not find us. They are not in these lands just yet."

Wolves interrupted her story again, and she paused to listen.

"But we are living in time day after day like Linears now?" a small girl whispered with concern in her voice.

"For now. While you are young and blossoming your Vechey talents, you must live in time. After fifteen winters, you will go through the ritual. It is—" Eterili poked the stick far to the left of the two time lines. "—here. Many, many winters even before when we are now. I will help you get there it is a very long time ago."

The children all exclaimed, "Wow!" "So long ago." "We can't see back that far."

"What happens next?" Eterili quizzed her pupils.

Wide eyes looked back at her.

She answered by poking the stick in the sand a making a small dot between the line for where they were now and main-time. "The universe pushes you out of time. You will no longer live it day by day like a Linear. You will arrive into your own moment, one not even as long as a blink of a firefly. There you will walk in frozen time that is only yours."

Their eyes got wider, and they all started to babble, "My Father says the shadows do not move." "My Mother says the flame stands still." "My Mother says you do not get dirty there, the dirt does not stick."

Eterili smiled slightly, cracked teeth showing, and nodded. "Yes, yes. Nothing moves save you. And from there you will then be able to see forward into main-time and backwards to the beginning of time if you concentrate hard enough. You will be able to move in out and out of time at whim."

They were silent, the children, each one imagining what the ritual might hold. How does the universe push them out of time?

Her voice interrupted their imaginations, "You will have a job to do."

"Protect time," the children replied in unison.

"Indeed," she said. "Every Vechey is pushed out of time and into their own place. You will tie into the earth itself, a place that will be your new home. The earth of that place will sustain you, though; you will need to go to main-time to feed. You will be scattered across the lands. The place that becomes yours, that is your place to protect time from…" She leaned towards the children waiting for an answer.

"The Manipulator." Their frightened whispers were barely audible.

"Every Vechey is placed to protect an area of land from the Manipulators who live in main-time among the Linears. Yes." She nodded and her attention wandered as if she was listening to the wolves. Though the children heard no wolves' call.

"They wear the Linears like a shawl," one child whispered to another.

Eterili's wet eyes looked at the children once more. "They inhabit a Linear's body until it dies then they crawl into the next living body that is close. Take care that it is not—" She leaned forward and lunged at the children with her hands while shouting louder, "—you!"

They squealed in delight and fell away from Eterili. She watched them run back towards their families then sat watching the fire dwindle. Eventually the sun threatened to rise. She rose and walked towards the large cave entrance where the Vechey lived. She cast one last look at the sky, a pink glow on the horizon, then walked into the cave's darkness.

# 9 FALL TO TRUTH

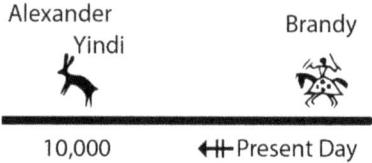

Alexander stacked the beams of wood near the edge of his house. Silently and efficiently he began framing in the extension. The work went quickly, and he smiled as the bathroom and bedroom began to take shape.

He enjoyed tasks such as these. It helped fill the eternity he lived in. Able to slip into any time and walk amongst Linears, he learned from them, gathered skills and honed talents while there. As much as he enjoyed sating his curiosity—he enjoyed even more returning to his home-time, in solitude, and creating things there.

He had built his house, here upon the mountaintop. It overlooked the valley spread out endlessly below. The wooden home was constructed directly atop his cave.

His favorite pastime was anything that worked with natural materials, woodworking and metalworking. Alexander ran his hand along the beams and considered his next steps. This extension would be like most of the house and have no electricity.

This had not been his original home. For thousands of years he had lived in only a hut, since his sleep cycles were spent in the cave. The hut only served as a place for respite between feedings, fixing things Yindi (the Manipulator) had corrupted, and waiting for the sun to rise in main-time (which would necessitate returning to the cave for sleep and drawing energy from the soil found there).

Eventually, he ventured to test his limits. He found by killing the Manipulator's host he gained time for himself. Eterili had warned against this behavior, stating it would occur naturally as the Manipulator had to inhabit Linears—and Linears die.

The first time he had killed the Manipulator's host, Alexander had watched to see how the Manipulator had found its next host.

Hundreds of murders had let Alexander explore his curiosity. He had traveled to far lands, even by boat. Eterili would have forbidden it. In her view of the way Vechey were to stay in their synced area—battle with the Manipulator, not kill the Manipulator—and exist. Battle to maintain time. Exist for nothing else.

Alexander explored, learned, brought those ideas back to his home here and battled with the Manipulator.

At first the Manipulator was just a foe to battle. They did not speak. He only thought of him as the Manipulator and for a thousand years the Manipulator never seemed more than a blind, need-driven being bent on destroying time, destroying Alexander, and otherwise showing no reason or thought besides mayhem.

Eventually, Alexander had grown bored and had done just as Eterili asked. He had stayed. Battled. Existed. How close had he been to madness before a Linear had crawled into his cave and he, like a fool, had fallen in love with her? Brandy: the reason for his current home-improvement projects.

Yindi had taken it as a personal quest to destroy Brandy once he had realized Alexander had feelings for her. Feelings for a *Linear*. Feelings for—*his food*.

Alexander slumped with shame. It was a weakness of his, not following the way. Eterili would not approve of his behavior.

Shame caused him to ignore the call to return to his hometime and find a mate. He found a mate once, promised himself to her. But that had been forever ago. Instead, he sat. Had that been the beginning of his darkness; the moment that he began to stop traveling, to stop exploring?

Alexander bent to move a medium piece of mahogany. He would use the wood for his next project. It was weightless in his frozen-time.

His parents would have probably been there at that moment waiting for their children to return home. All would have synced to that time, to that huge cave with its hundreds and hundreds of expansive passages and rooms. Father and Mother would have waited and it caused a pang in his nearly immortal heart to think of his mother worrying a stone in her pocket until it became as smooth as a river stone. Perhaps he should return anyway and explain to her his decision to part from the way, his sad affinity for Linears. It hurt him too much to consider what her reaction might be.

He sighed, a Linear affectation.

His mind pondered as he began splitting the logs to use as siding for the bathroom extension.

Thousands of years old and he still worried what Eterili and his parents would think of his behavior? Alexander smiled at the thought.

His smile faltered when a memory even furthered his shame of failing—when the Manipulator had inhabited his own body. It had been a horrifying matter of hours struggling to contain the beast until he spewed him out and locked him into the nearest creature: a toad, if memory served. Alexander had always been careful when he had killed the Manipulator except in a recent encounter when in anger, he had snapped the Manipulator's neck. Alexander had been so shocked at the emptiness when the Manipulator had left his dead host, Alexander had almost forgotten to let go of the corpse until it was too late and the Manipulator had crawled into Alexander's skin. It was an experience he did not wish to re-live.

He shook his head as if to rid himself of the memory and returned his thoughts to his task—considering how much longer this project would take him. He needed to complete this and then return to Brandy, his Linear love, after he rested first. It would take a great amount of concentration to slip into time exactly after he had left it. The thought of it set his teeth on edge. One mistake and he would hurt himself or Brandy. The thought of hurting her in such a way made his mood darken. Shame caused his cheeks to flush.

He had stood on the porch with Brandy, in an embrace. She knew nothing of his true existence. He had been caring for her and helping her heal by hiding her here in time at his home. The cause of her pain had been Yindi, the Manipulator. He had hurled Brandy under a bus. Alexander had tried valiantly and uselessly to adjust time himself to keep her from having to go through this pain. It had been useless. His only solution was to bring her here to his home only moments after he had finished it, 10,000 years before her time. Here she would heal.

Here she was temporarily hidden from Yindi. She would have to return to her time soon enough. Linears' minds synced and relied on the progression of time. If kept from their time for long, their minds shattered. Alexander worked at the chinking between the exterior logs as he considered the inevitable death Brandy would experience. It slowed his pace. Inevitable.

He would have to be careful. He had left her there on the porch. They had been intimate, their first time. The wood of the porch had been cool and hard to the touch. Her hair smelled of lavender. After months of caring for her and helping her heal, knowing he had limited time with her, every moment was a delight. This moment was the most sweet. There they had stood, ready to carry her back to her bedroom, then a random stray cat she had befriended had tripped him. He was falling with her in his arms. She was recuperating from a broken leg, arm, pelvis fracture, and skull fracture. She had been well enough to be with him on the porch—they had to work together to not cause her pain.

Then he was falling. In a blink, he disappeared. He needed a better position to save her from the fall. She had looked into his eyes as they had been falling, and he realized if he did this, removed himself from time and then inserted himself back again to save her from this fall, he would have to tell her the truth about his existence.

He had kept his true nature from her. She had seen his mouth frown as he had realized his time with her was over. He would have to tell her he was a Vechey and not a Linear and would have to explain the concept of what a Linear was.

She would either accept him or reject him. The moment he had avoided had arrived. He had disappeared and left her hanging there in space, falling, crashing towards the porch. The stupid cat had fled the scene, his manipulation done.

Alexander paused. How could a cat be in his time, 10,000 years before main-time and thousands of years before cats even came to this continent? Could a Manipulator have possessed the cat? Manipulators cannot travel through time. What brought it here and now? Or was it just chance? Were there others besides the Vechey and the Manipulators? Flustered, he brushed the thought away.

He had disappeared from their falling tangle of limbs, slipped into his frozen-time and saw the ghostly image of himself and her on the porch together, a passionate entanglement. Then standing. Then falling. Then he had disappeared.

She hung frozen in time, hanging in midair, eyes wide with surprise. He looked at her. His love. His *Linear*. Not the first time he had fallen in love with a Linear. Not the last time, he surmised, given his nearly eternal life.

The shame of it.

Knowing he would have to bare his soul to her when he synced back with time to catch her and keep her from falling to the porch, he had searched about trying to think of a gesture of love to give her. Flowers seemed to be too small. She was a practical person. An overage of floral arrangements would not soften the blow of delivering his story.

He turned from her ghostly face of shock. How to explain who he was, what he was to her? Why did he care? Alexander turned back to her face, because no matter how short his time with her—he loved her.

A thought occurred to him. She once spoke of the relaxation of soaking in a bubble bath. She said it was the one thing she missed most about her home and her time.

So here he stood, creating a bathroom with a marble floor and claw-foot tub and a bedroom that looked over the valley. If she hated him when she heard the truth about him, so be it. She would stay here in luxury until she healed enough to return to her time.

There she would die.

There the Manipulator would take her from Alexander. He touched the marble, stacked and waiting for installation, cold and smooth.

Once finished, he would sync back to time and catch her. Then he would tell her the truth about his existence. The syncing would be problematic and stressful. He had held her in his arms. He would need to sync back into time and not collide with himself or her. The moon had not been full, so his vision of time would not be as clear as if it was a full moon. It would be tricky.

Alexander touched the missing divot of his pinky finger and knew all too well the results of a syncing collision.

# 10 KEEP AWAY

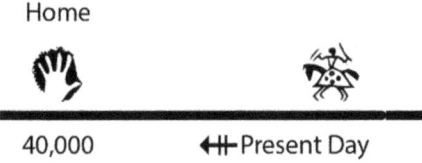

The sun had set hours ago. Eterili sat near the circle, ignoring the comings and goings of the younger children. They ran and jostled. Called out and hollered. Fell. Ran. Jumped. They did everything but sit silent and still.

As their activities brought them closer to Eterili they realized their proximity, perhaps warned off by her smell or her glaring eye, and promptly redirected their momentum away from her and kept up their jubilations.

The adolescent children, nearing ritual age, strolled across the ruckus trying to avoid the tumbling tangles of energy that were the younger children. Aithagg and his group were a year from their ritual age, fifteen.

Aithagg turned to Catha and whispered, "Can we talk?" He secretly handed an apple to her.

She hid the apple behind her skirt and eyed him suspiciously, then looked to Otski and Ygolz. They were busy discussing their latest feed, each one attempting to outdo the other's bravery.

"I was almost caught. I did not notice the spouse walking through the camp. He came into the tent and there I was," Otski said.

"Did you sync away in time? I froze once and couldn't move," Ygolz admitted in a rare moment of honesty. Remembering himself he added, "I wasn't seen though. Just before the Linear awoke, I synced away. I remembered to close the wound too before I left." Ygolz rubbed at his nose and looked down at the ground. "It did give me a scare though. I thought I was caught."

Catha leaned close to Aithagg and met his eye. She flicked her eye behind them, indicating for him to follow. Together they left the circle and the fire there. Finding secrecy in the shadows of a nearby tree they sat and leaned back against the rough bark. Their shoulders touched, and they sat together for a moment watching the tribe in front of them illuminated by the fire.

None of the group seemed to notice the two as they slunk to the shadows. The group continued to mill about cavorting and carrying on.

Aithagg picked at a stray piece of rawhide on his clothing. "We have to figure out a way to get you through the ritual." His voice was a whisper. He kept his eyes focused on the ground in front of him.

Catha pursed her lips tightly and sunk slightly before answering, "My parents talk of the others that did not make it. They think I can't hear them. But I do."

She looked to Aithagg. He met her gaze and held it.

"I have brothers and sisters who have not survived the ritual as well," he empathized.

"Not as many, I will bet." Catha dropped her gaze and continued, "so many of my brothers and sisters did not survive the ritual. They never could see through time."

"How many?" Aithagg touched her hand, a brief comforting touch.

"Fifty."

They both sat in silence neither wanting to expound on the fearful number any further.

Final Aithagg added, "I see." He paused then continued, "but not *all*." He squeezed her hand. "At least more than half made it through the ritual, right?"

"I suppose," Catha answered. "At least half made it through. The others disappeared into time and became Linears or," her voice trailed off then she whispered, "I don't know which is worse: being a Linear or dying."

Aithagg took her hand and held it tightly. "We need to come up with a plan. What if we snuck to the ritual site when the next group goes?" He turned to her, his eyes glittering with hope. "We could see the ritual and figure out an advantage for you—a way you can make it through the ritual even without." He paused not wanting to speak the truth.

"Go ahead, say it." Her words were sharper than she intended. Softening she completed his sentence, "Even without seeing time. It is a nice gesture, but how are we going to sneak to a place with everyone able to see through time? They'll see us and stop us. Do you know how difficult it is to get away with anything around here?"

Aithagg smirked. Having parents able to see through time made being a mischievous child very difficult.

They sat and considered options in silence. The darkness spread between them like a grim weight.

"I hate the way my mother looks at me," Catha said. "She looks at me as if I'm already dead or a Linear."

Aithagg leaned against her shoulder. "It must be hard to have lost so many over the years."

"My older brothers seem to fair better. I think they already saw through time by my age." Catha leaned back against Aithagg, leaning into his warmth. "I could just go away in the day. Wait for no moon here and a sunrise in main-time. Even you can't see through that."

"You are not wrong," Aithagg whispered and shifted to place his arm around Catha. She allowed it and pulled his arm closer.

"I'll just go and it will be easier on everyone." Her voice was resolute.

"Not easier on me." Aithagg ventured to kiss the top of her head.

Neither moved nor dared to speak any further. They watched the tribe in front of them carrying on with their evening activities as if the world was not ending. The children ran about the fire. The elders sat and spoke in low whispers. The adolescents, preparing for the upcoming ritual, tried to look unafraid. Their Shaman, Eterili, seemed to see all as she scanned the group in the dark.

Across the distance, Eterili's eyes lit upon the two huddled under the tree. They both straightened guiltily as if caught in a forbidden act. Aithagg removed his arm from around Catha's shoulders and brought his knees up to his chest. He laughed quietly to himself then whispered into his shoulder lest an elder read his lips, "Eterili, but she gives me the creeps."

They giggled together and then broke apart, making their way back to the campfire. As the two youths took their place in the warm fire's glow, they overheard fragments of conversations as various elders told tales to the children.

"…and before the sun could rise the wolf disappeared without a trace. Until this day you can still hear him howl as he looks for his next victim. Awooooooo." The elder lurched towards the children with his wolf's growl and they squealed in horrific delight.

No further talks of running away, finding a way to get around the ritual, or the plight of becoming a Linear filled the silence between them. Aithagg and Catha sat near each other quietly and eventually made their goodbyes as the evening slipped away and the sun threatened to rise.

***

Catha walked alone to her room. In their confined quarters, her parents' voices echoed.

"After the ritual, we'll go back to our home and things will get back to normal," her father's low voice grumbled.

"I can't go there anymore. To the fire." Her mother's sob filled the air. "I can't see them all—there."

Catha walked quietly hoping they would not hear her steps. She nearly ran to get by the passage to their room, her bare feet scraping on the cold rock floor.

She was undetected and collapsed into her domed room as soon she approached it. Tears did not fall from her eyes. She had cried her fill. Catha had no emotions left to give a loveless family who already saw her as dead.

She arranged her sparse belongings and silently calculated what she should take with her if she left the tribe. Absently she ate the apple Aithagg had brought her.

Catha was oblivious to dawn breaking. All else in the sprawling cave were quietly lulled into slumber by the pull of the sun as it rose. They would disappear and shift through time as they slept. Catha would simply lie on her soft pile of furs and sleep. She would not shift through time. She would not be pulled by the sun. She would only be trapped with time as it moved forward. Tears spring to her eyes.

A Linear. She was a Linear. She shivered in the cold and pulled the furs further around her. Hunger gripped her thin body in a tight fist.

***

After the sun set, Catha rose and found Aithagg walking the hallway outside of her cold, stone room.

"What are you doing here?" Catha asked.

"I've been up all day thinking about it. I think I have it figured out." Aithagg grabbed her hand and led her towards the opening of the cave. The cold darkness was pleasant and the warmer air of the evening pressed against their skin as they exited into the night air.

"What?" Catha asked but Aithagg cut her off.

"Not here. Wait."

Just then Otski and Ygolz ran out of the cave with a handful of younger children in tow.

"Give that back!" one of the younger boys shouted.

Otski threw a small, carved Mastodon tooth to Ygolz in an elaborate game of keep away.

"No fair," a youngster cried as he tried in vain to pluck the tooth from Otski's hands.

Otski feigned to the right so the youngster jumped right to intercept then Otski jumped to the left and threw the tooth further off into the woods. Laughing he called out to Aithagg, "Did you see that?"

Aithagg gave Otski a withering glare then stepped off into the direction of the tossed tooth. He returned within moments. He brushed the mud off the tooth displaying the carved symbols of the Eg'den clan: four wavy lines and a circle. He handed the soiled tooth to the thankful youngster.

"Spoil sport," Otski called out.

Aithagg looked at the youth softly, tousled his hair and said, "Go on now to eat. Make sure you have washed your hands. And that tooth. Your mother will have *your* teeth if you lose your clan's crest. It is not a plaything."

They watched the children run up the trail and disappear. Aithagg turned to Catha. "Come on. Let us go feed and then I will tell you what I have come up…"

He was interrupted by his parents appeared behind them.

"Are you going to help me strip the bark from the tree today?" Iskeho asked, a sly smile on his face.

Aithagg's face turned red and after a moment he answered, "I have other plans today, Father." He dared to glance at Catha. "If you leave it, I will get to it later. Promise."

Iskeho looked from Catha to Aithagg and then to Kei-tha. He smiled and cajoled, "I suppose I could be talked into staying near the camp and helping your mother with her beadwork and carving. She needs to finish the crest for your ritual, which will be here next year, before we know it."

Kei-tha snorted and shooed Iskeho away with a dismissive hand. "I do not want you underfoot. Surely you can help hunt game for the younger Vechey or something equally not in my way."

Iskeho held a small leather bag out for Aithagg. "Take this extra oil for your lamp. Come back well before dinner. You will be expected at the circle tonight for the parting."

"I will." Aithagg smiled at Catha. "We will."

The two walked away from the cave's entrance and down a secluded path. The parents watched them leave.

Kei-tha touched Iskeho's shoulder gently. "She isn't developing the traits. He is destined for heartbreak."

Iskeho patted her hand and held it to his chest. "He has to choose his path. The young know everything and think we know nothing." He kissed Kei-tha's cheek and added, "Were we not the same, those thousands of years ago when we ran through these same woods as we prepared for our ritual?"

"He is going to pronounce her and they will be bound. Then…" Kei-tha worried the stone in her pocket and did not finish the thought.

"We do not know that she will not survive the ritual," Iskeho whispered.

"So many of that line do not. He has to know. Aithagg cannot be bound to her. We have to prevent it." Kei-tha looked after the two who had disappeared from sight.

"You know that it would do no good." Iskeho tugged at Kei-tha's hand and led her towards the circle where the others were busy with the night's tasks.

He did not glance behind him though his heart longed to. Instead, he walked with his wife of twenty-seven thousand years and looked at the misty ghost memories swirling around them. It was haunting how crowded the air was with the thousands of visits they had made to this cave as a people. He saw himself as a youth, a teen, with Kei-tha, them after they had bonded, and them here with every offspring. The weight of so much time was oppressive at moments and he yearned to not see so much, to not remember so much, to find release from this burden. Such was not the way, and he turned back to his wife. "I can help you with the beads. I do a fine job."

"You will complain the whole time. But sit with me and we will enjoy the night."

\*\*\*

The teens walked further away from the group and turned to make sure they were out of earshot.

"Look, I plan on leaving when the sun rises and going to the nearby tribe of Linears. They will take me in." Catha lifted a bag under her shawl and showed it to Aithagg. "I've already packed."

Aithagg paused and then said, "I have come up with a way. You may not see through time, but you can move through it slightly. You are _not_ a Linear," he emphasized the word.

Catha seemed to shrink at the word Linear. "I am barely more than a Linear. I cannot feed. I can not see time." She drooped. "I can move through time, yes, a little. But what good is that if I cannot see where I am going. Useless. That is what it is."

Aithagg interrupted her, "What if I go there and mark a safe place where you can sync to and not collide? It would not be that hard at all." His words came quickly, urgently. "I will go to just after the ritual and take care to stay close to somewhere where one of the others stands. That way, my ghost image won't be seen. Just like when we used to play hide and seek. I will watch for a place where no one walks—where nothing moves and put a marker of some type. I think a circle of stones that you can see."

Catha started to interrupt him and he held up a hand.

"I will come back to this time and place a circle of stones. You may have to take small jumps to get there. Then you can get to the ritual site without fear of colliding with the—the thousands that have been there before."

"Listen to yourself. Thousands. Do you know how many have gone through the ritual throughout time? They all go to that site to do whatever the ritual is." Catha put the strap of her bag over her shoulder and hefted its weight with a stern shrug. "I have decided. I do not need you to save me. I will protect my family from the pain of facing me any longer and take my place as a Linear."

"I will follow the group tomorrow night when they go to the ritual site." Aithagg grasped her hand, and they walked down the path.

"Eterili will see. She sees everything," Catha protested.

"I do not know that she will. And if she did—what does it matter? We have all of time. We can go through the ritual and I can come back and put the markers there for you."

Catha considered the concept.

While they walked the moon crept higher into the sky and accompanied the stars. The night air was crisp.

"Do you know what happens at the ritual site?" she finally asked.

"The elders will not say. All that I can understand is that we gather around a fire ring much like we do here. But we have to move to a certain time forty-thousand winters ago and then from that moment we are pushed into our individual times where we will sync." Aithagg shrugged. "Then we begin our journey to find the place that will give us energy and begin our task of protecting time."

"The journey is long. Even those who can see through time do not always endure," Catha said despondently.

"But before then…" Aithagg placed both hands on Catha's shoulders and turned her to face him.

Just then, a small group of youngsters came running down the path. Exuberant squeals warned of their approach. The children ran past Aithagg and Catha.

"Last one there!" one of them shouted. The others were in hot pursuit.

Aithagg and Catha watched them go. She turned to Aithagg and said, "Let us do something with the evening then, if I am not going to run away and join the Linears." She smiled. "Let us go watch the stars in this near moonless night."

"What do you do if you can not feed on them?" Aithagg ventured.

"I take some of their food and eat as they do. As we did when we were young."

"Your parents do not notice?" he knew but asked anyway, hating to hear the answer.

"My parents have not tried to train me since I was young. They know. They ignore me and are waiting for me to…" A hitch caught in her voice. "They will not return to their time until after the ritual."

"Let us enjoy the night then and talk no more of this for now, shall we?" He held his hand out to her.

\*\*\*

A moon sliver sunk low like a glowing, grim grin. The fire reached towards it. All gathered round for the parting ritual. The adolescence of age would bid their farewells. Tomorrow evening, they would begin the trek to a distant place for the ritual. The parents proudly and worriedly stood at one end of the gathering area.

Iskeho held Kei-tha's hand, and they smiled gently to one another. He squeezed her hand encouragingly.

Eterili was unusually quiet and stood facing the fire. The heat shimmered around her and some imagined it magnified her stench.

As practiced, the Vechey of age filed in silently and stood around the circle facing the fire alongside of Eterili.

Those closest to Eterili braved the worst of her smell. She claimed to be as old as dirt and unable to tolerate water. The ancient one would anoint herself with oils and mysterious substances and had so for hundreds of moons. The anklets of canine teeth smeared with dried blood aided to the overall bouquet.

A drumbeat sounded slowly and methodically. The hollow thuds boomed from stretched hides beat with baton animal leg bones. Four such drums hid in the shadows. The musicians covered their faces with red ochre paint mixed with mud. It cracked and pitted. The shadows cast from the fire made the cracks seem to dance eerily like snakes across their faces.

All took their place and the beat of the drums echoed in the dark night. No one else made a sound. Even the insects seemed to wait in hushed silence.

*Boom.* The drums sounded.

*Rattle.* The teeth around Eterili's ankle.

*Boom. Thud.* The drums.

*Clink.* Dead teeth on dead teeth.

Only the youngest of the Vechey made any noise at all. They fidgeted at their parent's side, frightened by Eterili, the drums, the solemn adolescent and their long tortured shadows which seemed to shift and dance. The shadows seem disembodied, as if not cast by the youth at all. The shadows grew from the teen's heels as a writhing symbol of the change they would soon endure.

At once, Eterili turned from the fire and the drums stopped. Quietly, she called each adolescent by name. Her voice carried across the still night air. Each teenager turned their back to the fire when Eterili called their name.

Aithagg and Catha stood near each other watching the circle of teens older than them. Kei-tha searched the crowd till she laid eyes on Aithagg. She smiled gently when their eyes met briefly.

"What do you protect?" Eterili called out dramatically to the air.

"Time."

"Why?"

"Lest the sky pull my bones apart as the tribe is lost across all of time."

Eterili turned to face the fire again and raised both arms. "Have you heeded your teachings?"

"Yes."

"You are the next wave of Watchers. Sworn to protect time and keep it safe from the Manipulators."

"Yes."

"We will travel to the ritual circle where you will be pushed into your own time and away from all others."

"Yes."

One by one, the circle of teenagers turned away from their parents, their siblings, their younger friends, and faced the fire. They cast their eyes skywards and recited, "We will protect our time, the tribe, our Eterili. Lest our souls be rent from our bones."

Eterili threw something into the fire. It exploded into green flames. The green light flickered on their faces and then dwindled.

"It is the way," she said solemnly.

\*\*\*

The sun rose to a misting morning. Fog hung heavy around the trees. No one was there to see Catha shoulder her pack and without turning back walk away from the tribe's cave.

\*\*\*

Aithagg woke in the night. He hurried to see Catha outside of her room. As he approached the entrance, he sensed she wasn't there. The air was too still. He called out in vain, "Catha, are you awake yet?"

No answer.

He peeked in to see she had neatly folded the furs. The sound of his feet echoed coldly in the room. Aithagg looked in vain for a hint of occupation in the room, found none. He hurried to the front of the cave hoping he would find her there, knowing he would not.

He spotted Catha's parents seated nearby on a log. They did not seem upset or concerned. Perhaps they did not know yet. He moved on not wanting to alert them to what he only suspected.

Given the years of comings and goings it was difficult to see through all the visions of the past. Aithagg tried anyway. The sun bleached any movements during the day from his vision. He still tried, hoping to find a glimpse of which way she had gone.

Distracted, he did not notice when his mother approached. She stood directly before him, hands on hips, half grinning.

"Did you lose something young one?" she enquired.

"Mother." Aithagg tried to not look suspicious, making him look more suspicious. "I am waiting for the group. We will watch the ritual group depart."

"They have already left after sunset. You know that." Her smile widened.

"Oh I," he stammered.

She pulled him in for a hug. He tried to resist. She pulled him in even tighter. "I do not get many more of these before you take your ritual journey next year." She rested her head on his shoulder for a moment then stepped back, holding him with both hands at arms' length. "I suppose you have to go look for her." It was not a question.

Aithagg was truly shocked; he did not know his mother was aware. The shock showed on his face.

"You lovely mooning puppy, I am over twenty-seven *thousand* years old. You do not get that old without learning much." She squeezed his shoulders. "I have seen much, and this is not an uncommon occurrence."

Just then a group of small children went running by at top speed. A small amulet was being tossed between them high over the head of a shorter child who was shouting for them to give it back. An older, taller youth stepped in and stopped the shenanigans and gave the amulet to the younger child.

"I have to try," Aithagg finally whispered. "I can not just let her go without trying to help."

"Many have left, Aithagg," Kei-tha assured. "They do. They go to the tribes and live their lives in the sun." She tilted her head down. "That is the best outcome. The alternative." She smiled a sad smile leaving the alternative unspoken.

Aithagg pulled away. "So that is it? Become a Linear or die in the ritual? What type of choice is that?" He stood rigid then softened. He touched his mother's arm, remembering she had lost children to the ritual. "There has to be another way."

Kei-tha patted his hand. "You will only find rage in yourself if you do not find another way. It is what you must do. I fear you will only end up with a broken soul. Do not let this define you."

"I must try," Aithagg reiterated.

"Then you will need this." Kei-tha pulled a wrapped fur from off of her back and gave it to Aithagg. "Travel light and stay behind Eterili in time. After you find Catha, that is. You will not be the first to follow the ritual group in their journey."

Stunned and speechless, he took the pack from her.

Kei-tha smiled. "Come back to me. I get one more winter before letting you go to your own ritual."

They embraced, and she held on for a moment too long before releasing him.

Aithagg was already moving to the woods and away from the camp. "Thank you!" he called over his shoulder.

Iskeho approached Kei-tha and placed his hands on her shoulders. "Do you think I should follow?"

"And retrace your own footsteps when you set off to see the secrets of the ritual? Back when you were a whelp?" Kei-tha put an arm around him. "He has to follow his path."

They watched the moon rise and their 157th child run off into the woods as if he was the first one to have the thought of saving a failing Vechey who would become a Linear, the first one to sneak to the ritual site to understand its secrets.

"It is the way," Iskeho stated—wistfulness in his voice.

\*\*\*

The night held a slight moon, barely a sliver. Seeing through time was more difficult when the moon was not full. Aithagg had a guess she would have gone to one of the nearby tribes. There were few. Not being able to sync with main-time she would join a barely developed tribe and try to live amongst them. They might kill her on-sight for being different. Main-time's tribes, where he fed, were twenty-six thousand winters in the future. Those people were different more developed. They used different tools, had a small command of language. She'd be lucky to find a group in this time that would take her in. They wouldn't speak a language Catha would understand; he was sure of it. They themselves, the Vechey, had their own language separate from any Linear group they came across. The Vechey had developed as a people in an isolated pocket of time for thousands of winters.

He paused at the tree where they used to play hide and seek. He remembered the near miss when he almost collided with himself and she had kept his secret from the others.

There, he glimpsed her sitting near the tree recently. She had sat beneath the tree repacking a fur roll so it tucked neatly under her pack. Now that he had caught the trail, peering more closely he saw slight glimpses of her here and there. She had traveled off to the west. He assumed she was heading towards the river. If there were a chance of finding a tribe, it would be near the water.

He quickened his pace, following the trail until he found where she had camped for the evening. She was still there, asleep. The unusualness of it caused him to pause. Sleeping in the open. Vechey would die if they slept in the open. Aithagg covered his eyes, ashamed for being shocked at a non-Vechey trait of Catha's.

He sat next to her, afraid to wake her. How was he going to convince her to stay with him? How was he going to convince her to trust him to get her through the ritual safely?

Unable to aid her time-walking, she would have to shift on her own. He might show her safe places to stand where she would not collide with anything. She could do the rest. Then when their ritual time came, she could jump to the safe spots. When the push—the whatever pushed them into their personal frozen-time—came, she would get pushed along too.

Aithagg thought about it for a moment. He would have to figure out what in the ritual pushed the Vechey to their time. Something big, he surmised.

Then synced to her own time she would be safe. She wouldn't have to sync into time to feed since she did not feed. Things would be frozen in time, so hunting and gathering might be easy. How long would her life span last? Would she be a Linear out of time or a Vechey living as a Linear out of time? Is she immortal as he or a Linear? She has some abilities of a Vechey. His brain reeled trying to puzzle out the best solution.

Aithagg slumped. He looked at her sleeping figure; she must have been exhausted for she had not stirred at his presence.

What if their frozen time was further back during the long winter? The ice and cold had been abundant. Linear food was scarce.

Aithagg worried as the moon slipped by overhead and the stars dwindled in the night's sky.

Catha stirred and spoke quietly, "You worry so loudly." She smiled, the fur she lay upon half covered her mouth.

"We have to try. Let me try." He put a hand on her ankle, for he sat at her feet. "If it does not work, then you can run away to the Linears," he pleaded.

She sat up and rubbed at her eyes. "Aithagg, you are fighting the inevitable."

"What will you feed on?" He held out his hand to gesture to the woods about them. "There are barely any tribes in this time."

Crystal-clear tears sprung to her eyes, and she wiped them away angrily, upset at their appearance. "Remember, Aithagg, I am the *what* in your statement." She leveled a gaze at him. "I do not feed upon Linears. I. Am. A. Linear."

"Not really, though." He dropped his gaze. "You see a little through time. You can *move* through time." Aithagg brightened. "And most powerful of all you can walk in the day without pain." He tried to smile.

She did not return the smile. "Exile then. Alone."

He patted her ankle one more time, his thumb softly caressing the skin. Absently he looked off into the night's sky. "If you won't go to the ritual, let me get you to a time where there are tribes that you can fit in with. It is not safe out here on your own."

"Why not? You will go through the ritual and sync into your own time—alone. You will live your enormous amount of eternal days with nothing for companionship—alone. You have no worry for yourself in solitude. Why worry for *my* life alone?" Her words stung as she spat them.

"Things do not move in frozen-time. One is not prey there. There is no need to worry," he whispered.

She sat up and leaned close to him. "Fair point." She leaned her head against his shoulder. "I do not even know if I have the long life of a Vechey or the short one of a Linear. It is so shameful to be what I am that I cannot ask. I can glean no knowledge from the clan."

"I could find out." Aithagg sat up straighter. Catha's head bobbed forward with his weight shift. "I can go to the ritual site. I can follow your siblings. Find out what happens to them. Fifty or one hundred winters to look through for them. I can see if they lived the life of a Linear or a Vechey after the moment of the ritual."

"They did not survive," Catha stated matter-of-factly.

"Are we sure of that?" Aithagg challenged. "If they could not sync with time and continued on as a Linear would the tribe not declare them dead?"

She blinked and considered the options. "If the earliest one lived as a Linear he would have died by now. He was born a hundred winters ago."

"That will give us some information to go on." Aithagg bent and kissed the top of her head in his excitement. "Will you come back to the cave and stay with the tribe for now?"

"Why? You can go see the whole hundred years that have passed and be back to me in an instant. You are not thinking like a Vechey." She tilted her head up to look at him.

"I will have to be careful that Eterili does not see me." Aithagg considered.

"The group has already left. You will see them in time ahead of you. She will not be looking back over her shoulder." Catha reached up and placed a hand on the side of his cheek. "Come back to me and travel safely."

Aithagg looked at her upturned face. "I can only hope she does not look back. I can walk in the footsteps of the other travelers to hide in their ghost images. That should work."

She smiled and gave a half laugh. "You do not take hints well." She pulled his face close to hers and kissed him.

"I," Aithagg stammered, "suppose that I do not."

He held her close and their first kiss was awkward and sweet.

Catha sat up straight and away from him. "No matter what you find. Return and tell me the truth. I can not base my life on lies."

Aithagg mumbled a reply then stood unsteadily on his feet. Smiled crookedly. Disappeared.

Cold air collapsed into the place he had stood.

# 11 SECRETS

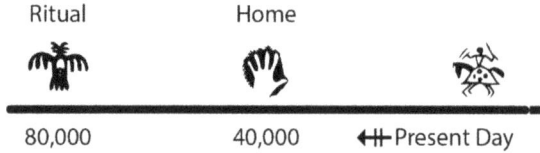

Eterili moved quickly for someone her age. She urged the adolescent group to move forward as fast as their legs would carry them. They had to move in-between time so they constantly moved at night. There was no safe place to slumber. It would take a moon cycle without sleep for them to reach the coastal land where the ritual site awaited.

The teens moved well and their enthusiasm for their destination helped them keep up the pace. The universe and time trudged along in its linear existence ahead of them. The ritual site they went to no longer existed even in their home-time. They would have to go back in time to when the ritual moment was forty thousand winters prior to their home-time. The teenage youngsters did not know why. They did not know what awaited them. Eterili followed. She urged them to go further, travel faster, keep moving.

The moon hung over them, an incandescent sneer.

Aithagg caught up to the group quickly. The trail ahead of him stood out as bright as the moon. Hundreds, thousands of

Vechey had traveled this path in the past ten thousand years and their ghosts filled the woods. He need not have feared being seen. The ghost images of travelers past were so thick it was like walking through an evening fog.

Absently, Aithagg wondered which one of these bright-eyed adolescents had been his siblings or her siblings. Which had lived? Which were doomed to die at the ritual? He brushed the thoughts away and concentrated through the mists of past travelers to find the most current travelers so he would not accidentally cross their paths. Surely, he was not the first to follow to learn the secrets of the ritual. A particular clump of ghost images ahead in the woods caught his eye.

A group had stopped here and gathered around a fallen comrade. The injured boy grasped his ankle and writhed in pain. There had been a commotion around the fallen young man and then Eterili had approached. She gestured, and the group fell away. One by one, they turned and left their friend. They looked over their shoulder, then turned and continued on their path towards the ritual site. Eterili inspected the boy's injured ankle.

Aithagg turned to look through the ghosts of the past to see what had caused the injury. He focused slightly so the images shifted and cleared but was careful not to shift into the time of the event. He saw the snake that had bit the boy. The boy had tried to hide the bite and continued on. It had not taken long, the pain must have become unbearable and then he had collapsed. Turning back Aithagg looked closer at the collapsed boy. The shell sewn into his tunic was marked with two square shapes: a relation to Catha, part of the Uakig clan. That would explain the snakebite. Snakes and smaller pests did not bother the Vechey. Linear blood, however, was food for more than the Vechey. This ancestor of Catha must have been as she was—not maturing, as a Vechey should.

In the mist images, Eterili had given the boy a small potion bag and then walked away. He had crawled to a nearby tree and sat without moving. He took the contents of the potion bag, consumed them, and then moved no more.

Aithagg stared until he shifted into the time and sat next to the boy's corpse. This was what death of his kind looked like. He considered, death to a kind that was more Linear than Vechey. Aithagg wrinkled his nose at the putrid smell. He shifted back to home-time to avoid the smell. The body had bloated and animals would come to eat at the soft parts first: the eyes, the throat, the lips. Then they would claw towards the bloated stomach. Rats would nibble at the fingertips and the end of his nose. The body would tip sideways and slump to the forest floor. Wolves would tear at the body with their sharp teeth. A larger wolf would take a leg while the smaller wolf pack waited their turn. The bits left by the wolf packs and birds would be covered in snow, then leaves as the seasons turned. The skin would dry and peel back. The jaw, already slack, would separate from the skull. The skeleton would crumble until very little was left.

Aithagg assumed this boy must have died over a hundred years ago. Perhaps he was one of the first of Catha's relatives. The newer images of ghosts appeared more opaque than the ancient ones. This boy's ghost was nearly translucent. His jawbone, nearer to Aithagg's own time, was less so.

Aithagg used his toe to stir the leaves where the body had decomposed through the years. He bent and used a stick to prod the ground. Focusing on now, he pushed the ghost images away. The object he sought birthed itself from the dirt. He picked it up and turned the shell over in his hand. With a thumb he pushed away the dirt encrusted on it. A double square insignia had been scratched into the shell's surface. It was pitted and weathered but still visible. He tucked the shell into a pouch hanging on his hip. When he returned, he would give it to Catha.

Eager to lose no time he hurried on and tried to ignore the falling of the Linears. Now he knew what the stages of death looked like and the bodies littered the trail in front of him. There were hundreds of deaths. Broken limbs. Attacks by large animals. Snake bites. Others slowed and weakened until they moved no more. So many like Catha who were not strong enough Vechey to survive.

Thinking on the eating habits of Linears he understood the deaths of those that weakened. They did not eat or would not eat food items, Linear food items, and did not keep pace with the Vechey who had fed prior to the trip. The Vechey would barely need sustenance for the month.

Aithagg paused at a gaunt, dead Linear. His eyes had sunken in and his cheekbones were gaunt. Aithagg had seen this in the tribes that had gone through a drought and had not enough food to sustain their life. How weak they were. How weak Catha must be then. Aithagg shamed at his thoughts.

A noise startled Aithagg, and he turned to find a familiar looking young Vechey standing near him. The youth looked at the dead Linear, which had attracted Aithagg's attention.

"You are not with the current group traveling to the ritual site," he said. His long wavy hair resembled Aithagg's.

"No. I am from further in the future. Trying to answer a question for a friend of mine." Aithagg trailed off not knowing how to describe his quest.

"Icaeph." The tall Vechey boy held out his arm in greeting. They grasped arms, hands locking at each other's elbows.

Aithagg hid his shock at knowing before him stood the brother who would face madness in the future. "Aithagg," he mumbled.

Icaeph looked at him for a long moment, studying the contours of his face. "I will not ask why you are here. Probably something Eterili would not approve of."

"Or why you are not with the group?" Aithagg smiled coyly.

"Well, there is that." Icaeph looked behind him towards where the other Vechey had walked. "I am taking a slight detour, that is true. I will catch up with them soon."

Aithagg did not question his brother's motives but instead looked at the ground, avoiding looking at a bulging sack slung over Icaeph's shoulder.

Icaeph shifted the weight of the sack then spoke, his words quick in an embarrassed rush of guilt, "There is a tribe nearby that I found. Usually the Vechey do not go to them. They are a small family. I found them a few years ago. Their elders were struck down with a disease and the children are the only survivors. I—"

Icaeph shifted the sack again this time to show it to Aithagg.

"—I bring them food so they survive."

"Do they see you?"

"No. I leave the bundle of food for them quickly and do not stay in their time long."

Aithagg considered for a moment. "Will you be able to return to them once you have gone through your ritual? You may be pushed far across this land from them."

"They are ready to be on their own now." Icaeph looked at the ground. "I know I should not care about Linears." His voice trailed off.

"Do you think Eterili knows?" Aithagg asked after a long moment of silence.

"Either she knows a lot and leaves us to our clandestine affairs or she knows nothing," Icaeph answered.

They sat for a moment in silence listening to the woods around them. Icaeph was the first to break the silence. "I need to return to the group and not test my luck with Eterili."

"I am going that way too," Aithagg admitted.

"It is not your time yet at the ritual though, is it?" Icaeph's eyes grew wide. "Oh, no it is not. Spying on the ritual to gain its secrets, are you?"

Aithagg smiled. "Not for myself."

He briefly explained the circumstances, relieved to unburden his secret. Icaeph nodded his head and did not seem to judge Aithagg for his plans.

"Let us journey together until you have to split away and hide," Icaeph invited.

They rose and began to walk together mostly in silence. Occasionally Icaeph asked questions about their parents and they joked about what stone, shell, or pig's hoof their mother might be worrying smooth at this very moment.

The trip was long and Aithagg began to tire. He was nearing the thirtieth moonrise. The landscape had changed drastically in the past ten moonrises. They traveled from mountainous areas into flat, grassy lands, which were slightly warmer and filled with flying pests. The air was wet and heavy, the ground soft, and the undergrowth was thicker than any he had seen. The stars hung brightly overhead. Aithagg worried. He would have to feed before his return trip. Were there tribes here in this swamp?

Before he considered the question any further the sight ahead of him stopped Aithagg in his tracks. They had reached the ritual site. It had to be the ritual site. Across thousands of years Vechey had gathered here in this area. Their ghosts formed a wall of white as they congregated around a central mass of white. Aithagg squinted, unable to see through it. Something had existed here forty thousand years ago and it was so large and powerful it erased all images before and after it in its wake. The Vechey had gathered around this central orb. They had all synced to the same time so they saw one another. Existed with one another.

Icaeph embraced Aithagg quickly and said, "I have to go join the others. It has been good to meet you my brother. Travel well."

Aithagg returned the embrace and stayed behind hiding in the tree-line. He watched Icaeph as he moved towards the group and then moved into the past. His movements became ghost-like. Other boys and girls he knew and had played with in the woods became ghosts of the past as they synced and stood with the ancestors. The first ancestors stood closer to the blinding white ball. The newer arrivals added to the crowd in concentric circles.

Eterili stood to the side, her back to Aithagg. She had raised her hands to the sky and had said something, gesturing to the bright light with her stick.

Then the group had stepped into the white mass. Eterili's pale silhouette walked towards the whiteness. Slowly she walked into the light.

Aithagg saw nothing of what transpired. They were there, then they walked into the white and disappeared.

Later in time, one lonely ghost image would emerge from the white light: Eterili. No one else emerged.

Drawn to the unanswered question of what was in the light, Aithagg crept closer. He marveled that Eterili seemed to leave only the one ghost trail. In looking around, he realized she only left her latest ghost trail as if her past and present were all one. It was perplexing. When synced into a time, such as they were in their home-time, they all left trails of where they had been—a veritable sea of Vechey trekking to this one spot. Eterili had led every trip. There should have been thousands of images of her leading the groups here. However, there was only the latest one. He shook the question from his head; tried to dislodge it from his brain. Why did she only leave the one trail? Where did everyone go? Why did no one return? Surely, he should have seen them come out as they synced to their own time and made their own path.

Aithagg inched closer and watched Eterili begin her solitary journey back through the woods towards home. She stayed in the past and did not sync to home-time. He was glad for it. It was less likely she would spot him. He did not know how much trouble he would be in if she caught him. He would much rather not find out. The air was thick and oppressive against his skin.

Aithagg looked back toward the light. He needed to find answers before returning to Catha.

At this point, what could he tell her? Nothing. He found one of her clan who had died of a snakebite. There were probably others he witnessed in the hundreds of deaths he had seen along the trail to this ritual site. Then he watched everyone join into one moment in time, walk into a ball of white as opaque as milk, and only Eterili stepped out. Eterili left no trails of history, no trace of where she had been, as if she had only traveled the one time, the latest time to this place. His head reeled with unanswered questions, none of which would help Catha know more about her future. He had to know more.

Aithagg stepped closer to the ball of white intent on giving it a closer examination. Would Eterili see him? Would she see the ghostly image of him moving closer to the ritual or would she pay him no mind? Was he another moving shape in the middle of thousands? He hoped for the latter.

He walked through the throng of misty-ghosts-of-Vechey-past who had stood upon a solid patch in the middle of swampland. The ground was mucky and sucked at his moccasins but was not as stagnant or murky as the shin deep water he had waded through earlier in his travels. This ground rose from the marshland and stood as a dry respite from the murk. Its width was ten large-tusked-hairy-beasts by twenty lined up tusk to tail. In the center sat a clearing, at the edges—dense undergrowth and gnarled trees.

The white ball of light was massive. Its brilliance was so bright, even in the past it made Aithagg squint to look at it. It was taller than the tops of the trees. Upon close inspection, he realized it wasn't a ball at all. It was more like a long streak coming from the sky and then erupting into a blaze here at the ground. The streak from the sky was less bright than the brilliance of the central mass of light. The sphere of light itself filled the open field.

Aithagg walked towards it and directly into the white light—though he stayed in his home-time and did not dare travel back to when this light had occurred. His teachings informed him it had happened about forty thousand winters ago.

The white was all encompassing, and he imagined it shut out all sound as he walked into it. He held his hands up to shield his eyes from the brightness. Inside, only the whiteness existed. It shone brighter than anything and rivaled his memories of what looking at the sun had been like as a child. He turned slowly in circles to find any of his tribe as they had stood here in the past. He saw nothing but the brightness.

"What are you doing here?" Eterili crooned softly.

He turned, in vain, to find where the voice came from. She was nowhere to be seen. He stood firm and returned a question, "Why do you have only one ghost trail as if you only exist the once?"

A soft chuckle echoed to him from the whiteness. It swirled around him. He tried not to panic. Blood red sweat beaded on his forehead.

"Curious one," she croaked. "Unusual. I do not see many this brave or this idiotic. Looking for clues to tell your little Linear friend?" Eterili appeared out of the whiteness in front of him. Her bent visage hunkered slowly in his direction.

Aithagg held still and tried to stand at his full height. He chose to be honest. "I am. I do not know if she will live a near eternal life of a Vechey or the short one of a Linear. If I could give her that answer, she may decide to stay with the tribe."

"With you, you mean." Eterili slowly ambled towards Aithagg and stopped three lengths from him.

"No," he denied his intentions might be slightly selfish. "I only intend to help her."

"You already have your answer. You refuse to realize what you have seen."

Aithagg puzzled for a moment, recalling the hundreds of dead along the trail to the ritual site. "The Linears die along the way, weak and unable to keep up the pace."

"What else did you see?" She took a step closer.

"The strong Vechey assemble here and as one enter this." Aithagg held his hands up. "They come to this place and disappear into the light. Only you return."

"This is true." She took another step closer.

"You only leave one ghost image as if the last time you went through is the only time. I do not understand," Aithagg continued.

Another step brought Eterili closer to Aithagg. She stood one body-length away. Her musty smell permeated Aithagg's nostrils. Though he did not need to breathe air, he still drew breath enough to smell things around him and speak. He stopped this insignificant breathing to avoid the stench.

"You may never understand it. I am the oldest Vechey and no longer sync with any time. I am my only time," she said.

He tilted his head to one side gauging the distance between them and wondering if she would strike. Would he be able to overthrow her?

She took a step and the anklets of teeth clacked about her, singing a solemn song of mayhem and death.

"She will not survive the ritual even if she makes it to here," Aithagg spoke quietly as if to himself. "I do not know what happens here in this whiteness, but I do not think she will be strong enough to survive it. She will die, most assuredly."

"This is also true." Eterili stilled and came no closer.

Aithagg ran a hand through his curly, dark hair. "I have to try to help." He looked down. The whiteness blocked out the ground, hid his feet. He stared for a moment, disoriented, then continued, "She can not die alone." Looking up he into Eterili's midnight black eyes he asked, "It is not the way, I suppose?"

"What you must ask is are you trying to save her so you avoid heartache? Or are you thinking about her?" Eterili took one small step towards Aithagg.

Preoccupied with indignation, he did not notice. He raised his head to answer, "I am thinking of her. Is it selfish to want to save her? Protect her?"

"Are you bound to her?" She asked quietly.

He answered too quickly, sounding like a sulking child, "No."

Eterili raised a bony finger and pointed at the young boy's chest. He imagined spiders must hide under her fur shawl. The gnarled finger quivered and its generous filth looked hardened. The nail was twisted, thick and dark with, he imagined, a putrid substance. The digit came slowly closer to him. He stood parallelized. Aithagg smelled her more clearly now: dirt, mud, blood, dead flesh, excrement, sweat, worms, an undertone of death—the smell of a rotting deer's corpse baking in the sun from his youth.

Her filthy finger hovered a hair's width from his chest and she whispered in a low voice, "I am the beginning and the end."

When she touched his chest with her dirt-stained fingertip, an electric shock went through him like a bolt of lightning. His ears rang and the whiteness, which had been around him, burst from within. Searing heat and freezing cold all at once exploded in every cell of his body. He opened his mouth to yell but no sound would come forth. Darkness washed over him and in a faraway distance he heard Eterili's words, "It is the way."

Then.

Darkness.

***

"—agg?"

He struggled to open his eyes. Someone from far away shook him. A powerful ringing impaled his ears.

"Aithagg?" The voice was insistent and started to cut through as the ringing diminished to a loud thrumming.

He tried again to open his eyes and found they would obey if he insisted.

Catha hovered over him; her long hair brushed his face. Absently he touched a long dark lock then he touched her face almost in wonderment.

"Dreaming?" he whispered.

"Not that I am aware of. You appeared back here seconds after you left. Except that you were asleep or unconscious at least." Catha brushed her hair behind her ears.

Sitting up was a struggle and Catha assisted him to an upright position. She eyed him then ventured, "Eterili saw you."

He nodded his head. "I found no answers—only more questions."

"I feared as much." She held his hand in hers and they sat in silence.

"I have no formal gift to give you." Aithagg turned towards her in a rush, intensity in his voice.

She frowned slightly, anticipating his thread of thought.

He pulled the shell from his pocket. Its double square etching was visible in the lantern light. "This is from one of your first siblings." He held it out to her. "I promise myself to you if you will have me."

She stared at the shell for a long moment.

Aithagg hesitated. "I should go carve a totem myself and bring it to you." He paused as if to leave and she stayed him with a hand.

"Do not." She took the shell from him and turned it over.

He explained the origin of the shell as she inspected it, her eyes never leaving the double square etching.

After a moment he fell silent waiting for her answer. She had become still while gazing at the ancient totem.

"Stay and we will face the ritual together. I cannot tell you what will happen or how to prepare for it. I will stay with you and protect you." He smiled, hopeful.

"To promise yourself to me is short sighted, Aithagg." She held the totem up as proof. "I will die like the rest."

"You do not know that." He tried to take the shell from her saying, "I was not thinking. This is a wrong gift of promise. I should."

She cut him off by hugging him tightly. "No, it is perfect," she whispered into his shoulder. "It is the truth of me and only you have ever risked everything to show me the truth. I do love you."

Surprised at the turn of events, Aithagg held her as she broke into tears. He was unsure of what to do and merely held her while she cried on his shoulder. Eventually, the tears dried.

She placed the shell in a bag tied at her waist. She patted it as if content on its placement. "I will have to find a Linear tribe in this time that I can be with or get through time to a Linear tribe. You cannot be promised to me. Nor I to you. It is not wise."

"If it comes to that, I will help you get there," Aithagg stated resolutely.

"And if it does not come to that?" She asked coyly.

"We will go through the ritual to sync in a time together and live as a unit." He dared a smile. "I will help you get through time if you need it."

"Do not flatter me, we both know I will need a lot of help to move through time blind to it as I am." She pulled at his hand to help him stand next to her. "You are a hopeless one." She tugged at his arm and he enfolded her in an embrace.

"We must announce that we are promised to Eterili and our parents. Eterili already suspects." Aithagg gathered Catha's fur roll from the ground and shook it out. "She knows everything. We were deluding ourselves to think otherwise."

"You saw nothing of the ritual?"

"Only a gathering around something and then—nothingness."

"No one came back out that you could see?"

"I suppose it is a portal of sorts from which she can push everyone to a specific place and time. As she pushed me here." Aithagg cringed. "With her bony finger."

They gathered the rest of her things and headed back through the night towards their tribe's cave, arriving just before dawn broke. No one questioned their sudden arrival or the collection of obvious travel things she held in her hands. Both returned to their sections of the cave as if it was any other day.

They both slept fitfully, plagued with the impossible dreams of being together in their own frozen-time.

# 12 A LOOMING PRECIPICE

*Drip.*
*Drip.*
*Drip.*
*Drrrrip.*

*Drip.*

Icaeph listened to the distant water drips. He awoke slowly realizing he must have synced with time again to hear water dripping, things moving. Time. He was in it. What was he thinking before the water awoke him? Rolling onto his side, he touched the dirt floor of the cave absently. The cold comforted him.

Unknown to Icaeph in a distant time, a group of adolescent teens were gathering around a fire and going through their parting ritual. They were preparing for the travel to their ritual which would propel them through time to their own moment where they would sync and stay forever.

He rolled again onto his back. Icaeph's mind turned to his own parting ritual. In that past he had not been able to recall the details. Yet, now, he saw the event as if it were unfolding before him.

He had taken his place at the circle. His mother sat at the fire and tried to put a brave face on. Icaeph clearly saw the worry she tried to hide. She had her hand in her lap—worrying something in her pocket: a stone or a shell. Icaeph had smiled bravely and grabbed the hand of his promised. Brevni stood close to him and she beamed with pride and happiness. She had turned to him and said something.

Icaeph's smile faltered. What had she said? He frowned, trying to remember. Water in the distance dripped, bringing Icaeph back to the present.

Brevni. He had not thought of her in thousands of years. She had been everything to him, strong and brave. She had made a token woven from plant fibers for him. Two nights before the parting ceremony, she promised herself to him and presented to him the gift. Brevni. The woven necklace had disintegrated over time.

*Drip.*

*Drip.*

Icaeph sat and stared into the darkness. He tried to recall her face. They had lived here for a while. She had lived here with him. Together they had kept time running its course despite the Manipulator's attempts at pushing it. It had been a slow cat-and-mouse game as there was not much to force time off its tracks. The isolated tribes moved across the lands. Keeping them moving and interbreeding, exchanging skills and ideas was the only thing necessary. Thousands of years had rolled by and he and Brevni had been...

*Drip.*

*Drip.*

Had they been? Icaeph stood and listened to the outside world with all his might. Was the Manipulator out there? No. Still stuck in the deer, he hoped. He might have some peace for a while until the Manipulator found a host. Given the sparse population, when he trapped the Manipulator into an animal, it might take a hundred or more years before the Manipulator came near a human host again. Peace for Icaeph. Peace for all.

What had he been thinking about? No Manipulator for a hundred years. Had Brevni been here with him? He realized he was standing at the opening of his cave with no memory of walking here. The sun had set. Would his mind wander so much he would walk out of the cave into the sun? Icaeph hoped not. Absently he stood and stared at the moonless sky. Was this main-time or some other time between now and then?

Brevni had been here with him. He was sure of it. How long, though? How long before she...

He refused to think about when he had lost her.

Raindrops fell outside and dripped from the rock opening of his cave.

*Drip.*
*Drip.*
*Drip.*

Icaeph held a cupped hand out and gathered water in his palm. He watched it drop there, mesmerized by the ripples on the water made by each raindrop.

The sun was almost rising. He had stood there in the cave's opening all night, staring at the water in his hand.

This must be madness, he thought to himself, unable to remember what he had done all night. He turned back to his darkness and disappeared from sight as he synced back to his frozen-time.

Hidden in the brush, a deer stood watching the entrance to the Icaeph's cave. Her ears twitched as each sound echoed through the woods. The Manipulator raised the doe's head to sniff the air, searching for Linears: in the distance, something burning, they must not be far. The-Manipulator-inhabited-doe began walking through the woods to find a new Linear host. Along the way, the doe stopped at a field of fragrant purple flowers. There she paused and took in the sight until the raw need of finding a Linear erased any momentary twinkling of peace.

# 13 THE PROMISE GIFT

Home

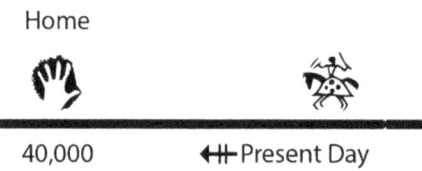

40,000          ⊬Present Day

"Where did you get that?" Her mother's voice was shrill and needling.

Catha looked up from her quiet place by the fire where she had been trying her best to be invisible.

"It was a gift," Catha stated quietly.

Her mother, who had not so much as spoke to her let alone look her way for over a month stared at her with burning eyes. "From who?" She came closer and stood over the girl.

Catha looked up and leveled a gaze at her mother. She did not answer the question. She returned the shell to the pouch at her hip and patted it.

"I asked you who that came from. You will answer me." Her mother's voice was piercing. She took a step closer and reached to grab Catha's arm.

"It does not matter," Catha whispered as she stood. "I will leave soon and you can return to your time."

"I made that," her mother insisted and moved aside as Catha stood. "I inscribed that. It is not yours to have. I gave it to our firstborn."

Catha bit back the comment she wanted to spit, how her beloved son had died by snakebite because of his Linear smelling blood. How Aithagg had found the shell and given it to her as a promise gift. How she would leave and start her own time and live where someone loved her and did not look at her as if she had already died. How she might for a moment not be ashamed for her Linear leanings. She might just be herself and be free.

Catha said none of these things. Instead, she softened towards her mother and patted her shoulder. "It must hurt to have lost so many."

She walked away and saw her father standing near. His grim stance and crossed arms said all she needed to know. She approached him. "I will move my things and be nearer to the next ritual group. You two need not stay. I absolve myself from you. You can return to your time and be free of me." Catha placed her hand on his chest. He did not react. "You two have no love to give and I have none to return. It is best to go on our own paths now. I am sorry that I am not be what you needed."

She walked away from the fire and into the darkness. When she returned that morning, her parent's room was vacant. They had placed extra furs from their room onto her bed. She supposed that was as much love as she had ever seen from them.

Aithagg appeared in the doorway. "They have gone?"

"Yes. It was best." She sank to the floor and brought her knees to her chest.

"I did not see you all night." Aithagg sat near her and also put his knees to his chest. "I assumed that you wanted to be alone."

"Mmmmmhmmmmm," she mumbled.

"We should announce our promise to my parents and Eterili tomorrow at the evening's fire ring." He kissed the top of her head. "It is not long until we depart for our ritual. A few moons, perhaps."

"We can walk through time, most of us can walk through time. Why do we have to wait?" She moved her arm to entwine in his and rested her head upon her knee.

"I always supposed it was because Eterili leads the groups to the ritual site and she must rest between each trek. It is a moon cycle there and another one back." He leaned his head upon her arm resting in his knee. Their noses nearly touched. "She is as old as dirt." He kissed the tip of her nose and she smiled. "Your nose is cold."

"I feel the cold more than you do."

He pulled one of the extra furs from her pile and placed it about her shoulders. After fussing with it to stay in place, he returned to his position of being nose to nose with her. "There."

"You should stay." She glanced over her shoulder at the mount of furs. "Keep me warm." Her face flushed with slight embarrassment.

Aithagg smiled gently. "Are you sure?"

"That I will be cold. Absolutely. I shake with the cold every night," she answered.

"Are you sure that you want me to stay here?" Aithagg clarified.

She rolled her eyes. "You do not take hints nor sarcasm very well."

"I suppose that I do not." He bent to kiss her, and she met him with warmth.

They fumbled together in a first, sweet encounter leaving them both warm despite the cool air. Sleep overtook them and with limbs entwined, they both disappeared.

***

Searing pain as bright as the sun awoke Aithagg. He leapt from the bed. Realizing his left hand was the center of the shocking pain—he cradled it protectively to his chest. He quickly checked to make sure Catha was unharmed. She slept quietly, her eyes barely visible from underneath the pile of furs.

Aithagg inspected the source of the intense pain: the small, pinky finger on his left hand. At the end of the finger a divot of flesh was missing. What remained was a smooth indentation of raw, cauterized meat. He stared at it in disbelief.

Catha stirred and poked her nose over the furs. "Are you all right?" She sat up quickly, the furs falling from her naked form. She pulled them back with one hand to cover her modesty. "We fell asleep! You would have shifted through time. We're not bound yet to shift through time together as we sleep. We could collide. I didn't think about that." She pointed at his finger. "But wait, I do not shift in time. I do not think I shift in time." She considered.

Aithagg held out his finger to her. "You shift! You must have shifted through time. Last one there wins, remember? You must have collided with me." He bounced onto the furs next to her and winced as pain jolted through his finger.

"Does it hurt much?" she asked.

"Only a little," he lied.

"So, I shifted and collided with you. How odd. I did not think I shifted as I slept."

"How would you know if you did?"

"True point. Do you not wake up in other times, sometimes, if a noise awakens you?" She inspected the finger.

"I have only done that a few times. It is most disorienting."

"I would assume so." She kissed around the wound, which looked angry and red.

"That means you must have more Vechey traits than you think. Perhaps your skills are only late in blossoming?" Aithagg was hopeful.

She dared to be hopeful. "When we are bound then, we will shift together and after the ritual we will sync together." She kissed the palm of his hand and then his chest. "I might see through time yet. Oh, that is such a relief." She kissed his soft neck, and he pulled her closer.

Their second encounter was more educated and filled with a passion fueled by hope and dreams.

# 14 HOPE

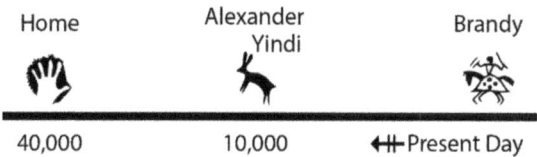

Alexander looked over his handiwork. The marble bathroom and bedroom extension gleamed. Tired from the effort, he would have to feed soon and rest before returning to Brandy. Before he returned to her, he would heat a cauldron of water and fill the claw-foot tub. How out of place it all looked here in his time before modern amenities. This house would crumble to dust in a few hundred years and disappear into oblivion. He had no concern since he inhabited the house mostly in his frozen moment. These scant few months he had spent synced with time and Brandy had been the only moments he had witnessed the house at all as it sat through the weather. He was happy his work on the house held and he had made the dwelling sturdy.

Alexander wondered if she would accept him and his story of who he was. What a Vechey was. What a Linear was. He closed the door and walked through the long corridor towards the front porch where Brandy would be falling. He hoped she would not reject him. A portrait hanging on the wall caused him to pause.

Catha. It had taken him a thousand years to paint this first portrait and hang it on the wall though it hurt him every time he looked at it. They had held such hope for their future together. He smiled at the memories he had of her. A shell with its double square engraving sat encased at the bottom of the frame in a glass box. Next to it, a gleaming polished stone and a small engraved rock.

So long ago, Alexander thought to himself, so very long ago.

# 15 PROMISED

Home

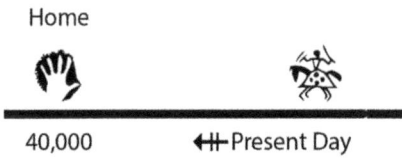

40,000     ⊢⊢Present Day

Catha had known for a while she would not pass the ritual. It was impossible. She watched as the other Vechey children her age played hide and seek through time to help sharpen their time syncing abilities and stretch their skill of seeing. She saw little. Otski and Ygolz jumped through time with ease. Aithagg: he hid it, but he saw further than any of them. He kept distant from everyone, never sharing much, not showing his capabilities. He was unlike Otski, who boasted at everything he did. She noticed, Aithagg would even set Otski up to win. He would pull back and let Otski win at hide and seek, or other games they played so Otski could boast. Aithagg did not need the win. He was content in knowing he was able to but did not. She doubted her reasons for loving him even though she loved him more for that simple character trait. Catha thought long and hard about why she had stayed close to him. Perhaps it was the way he propped her up. He saw the good in people and believed in them. That was something she had never experienced with her parents. She understood the draw towards someone that gave her a feeling she had not known. Is that love? Is that something that could sustain for an eternity? That is if she made it through the ritual, something she doubted very much.

So many of her siblings had not made it through the ritual. So many that her parent ignored her, treated her as if she were already dead. She did not fault them for it. They had built up a wall around themselves to avoid the pain of losing another child. Her lonely heart broke. Why did they continue to come back to the home-time and procreate if they doubted the child would live? Then, they did not love the child even for the short time they were here? Why? She took a deep breath, reusing to fuel the anger brewing in her lest it blossom into deep and eternal bitterness.

Catha didn't understand her parents. They had all of eternity with each other in their own frozen-time far away from here. They had traveled far from the ritual site. Her father, in the rare times he spoke more than a grunt, spoke of how they had traveled across the mountains, sleeping temporarily in caves until they came to the far northwest. There they synced into their place and time together. Their cave overlooked a large valley and their time was nearly at main-time. He missed it. He longed for the quiet.

Catha understood the longing for quiet. She often secreted away in the day, so she might enjoy peace with her own thoughts. She could be herself with Aithagg. He was like a safe, warm blanket. He did not look at her as a failed Vechey. He saw more in her than she thought existed. She had tried to run from everything and he had followed her. He had tried his best to find a way through the ritual for her. Perhaps they would work, perhaps not. Either way, she decided to not run from her potentially short life. She would own who she was. So what if she was not showing all the traits of a Vechey? So what if she might not be strong enough to see through time, to survive the ritual?

She refused to adopt her parent's outlook on life. She would return the hope Aithagg gave her. She would give everyone else that same hope. She had nothing to offer, she thought. She could not hunt well for the food the small ones needed. She could not move silently and could not see the through time as the hunters did. They found the prey so easily.

Instead, for many years she walked during the day to find beautiful plants. Her favorite memory was finding a vast field of purple flowers. She had spent nearly the whole day walking amongst them and carefully taking cuttings to cultivate in her growing garden. Though she did not think about it, she seemed drawn to where the most amazing blossoms were. She would find fruit budding on small trees, berries on vines, flowers in bushes. For many winters she had brought back cutting after cutting and established a garden near the cave's main entrance; the cave system itself had multiple entrances. Here she would enjoy trimming, cutting, grafting, testing, seeing what made the plants grow and harvesting the fruits and vegetables. Since she did not feed as a Vechey, this was a great benefit to her and to the children as well who had not yet learned to feed. It made her happy, and many turned a blind eye to it knowing she must walk in the day to tend to her garden.

She had woken up early one evening before the sunset to harvest a crop of blackberries. There remained plants untaxed by the local wildlife. She wanted to bring them back for the small ones. She filled a basket she had weaved from pine needles and wet branches. The sun painted the sky with brilliant pinks and oranges giving away to deep purples. She sat on a nearby rock, the basket of berries in her lap, and enjoyed the sun as it left.

"Found you," Aithagg whispered from behind her.

She turned to see him approach. He had wrapped himself in furs completely from head to toe, not one inch of skin was visible.

"That is brave for you to come out here like that. How did you know it would work?" She scooted over leaving a room for him to sit next to her on the rock.

"I questioned Eterili until she answered me about the sun." Aithagg sat next to her and leaned against her shoulder.

"Of course you did." She leaned against him.

"Where did you learn to do that?" He gestured with a fur-covered hand.

"Well, I did not ask Eterili about it." She smiled. "When I was very young, I picked a flower to give to my mother. I grabbed the roots and everything. I wanted her to have a flower."

"Did she take it?"

"She did. She told me to leave the roots in the ground next time so the flower might continue to grow more." Catha snaked her arm under the furs, careful to not expose Aithagg's skin, and found his hand to hold. "That got me to wondering if they would grow if I replanted the roots. So I did. And it bloomed."

"I do not think about plants much."

"Most of us do not. I looked for the pretty ones first and then found the ones Eterili had said were safe for the young ones to eat. Why not have our own crops here instead of having to travel out to find them?"

"True."

"It keeps me busy."

"Indeed."

They sat in silence for a while and the sun set. After the last light had faded from the sky, Aithagg shed his fur armor.

"That is better." He smiled in relief.

"We will need to get back soon." She looked over her shoulder. "Will your parents not look for you?"

"Not really." He shrugged. "My mother knows where I am at all times whether or not I tell her. It is like she can see through time or something and find all my comings and goings."

"Something like that, I suppose," she answered.

The silence filled the air around them and they enjoyed watching the stars light up the sky one by one.

Catha finally turned to Aithagg and handed a small wrapped present to him. She had made the wrapping from woven plant leaves and tied it with a rope braided from long grass blades. Flowers adorned the top.

Aithagg turned the beautiful package over in his hands. "I have never seen anything like this."

"I made the wrapping." She beamed from ear to ear. "Open it. It is my promise gift to you."

He kissed the top of her forehead and looked at the box again, unsure of how to begin.

Catha tugged on a loose strand which tied the package together. It unfurled the wrapping. Inside was a deep garnet gemstone. It was smooth and polished. The stars reflected across the surface.

"I made a rock pool in the waterfall and put the gem there. It rolled and tumbled until it became smooth!" She picked it up and turned the gemstone in the starlight. It fit into the small of her hand.

"How long did it take?"

"About three moons."

He paused and looked at her, mentally calculating. "That is before I gave you the shell. That sad excuse for a promise gift."

She patted his arm. "It is the perfect gift and you know the reasons."

He took the gem from her and held it between his eye and the moon. "This is amazing. The most beautiful thing I have ever seen." He looked into her eyes. "Not as beautiful as you."

She rolled her eyes at him. "That is a tired line." She kissed him quickly. "But say it again."

"Not." He placed a hand behind her neck and gently caressed her cheek with his thumb.

"As." Aithagg placed his other hand behind the small of her back and turned her towards him. The gem carefully held between their hands.

"Beautiful." He leaned in close and looked deeply into her eyes.

"As you." His lips met hers with deep passion.

A bounding bunch of youngsters interrupted when they ran by yelling and scrabbling towards parts unknown. The two teens watched the children run by and then their chaperones after them.

"We will come back and have children of our own and raise them here," Aithagg said.

She smiled sadly, the corners of her mouth turning down. "I do not know. I would hope that we do." She frowned even more. "But."

"Do not think it. Do not go down the path of disbelief." He tried to make his voice gentle and did not add for her not to think like her mother, which would be cruel. "It could happen. Imagine how wonderful that would be."

She nodded and joined in with his reverie. "You could teach them how to take the bark from a tree and create benches from it, or tables, or boxes or all the things you and your father have done with wood."

He smiled. "You could teach them how to grow things. Flowers and plants and fruits and things for the animals to feed on."

She darkened for a moment.

He added, "And the young ones. But I am thinking of our eternity where we do not need the fruit and food, really. That is no reason to not have it. You can grow all types and all the beings that eat of it will be better for your garden."

"Such smooth talking," she chided.

Aithagg chuckled and pulled her closer to him.

The night sang its music to them via croaking frogs and chirping grasshoppers. A nearby coyote howled.

"What will we do for all of eternity?" she whispered.

"I do not know that it is all of eternity," Aithagg answered quietly. "Only Eterili is as old as the world." He pulled her head under his chin. "True, those that make it through the ritual are all here today, mostly; those that do not go the way of madness. Hardly any of us die like we see the Linears and animals do. But I do not think it means we do not die."

"You ruin good moments. I meant—"

Aithagg cut off her words. "I know what you mean. And I think too much. Brood too much. Mother calls me an old soul." He hugged her tightly. "I apologize."

"Do not."

"I do."

"You should not."

"Why?"

"You accept me as I am. As I do you," she whispered.

Aithagg had no answer to this, and they fell into silence again. The stars shifted in the sky above them.

"We should join the others at the fire ring. Perhaps the elders will tell their stories. I like to hear them." Aithagg helped her stand.

Together they walked hand in hand towards the fire.

\*\*\*

The usual group was around the fire pit. The elders were there telling stories and keeping the younger ones entertained.

"How long have you been here?" Aithagg asked the elder D'olr.

The "older" man, who looked like a Linear would after sixty moons, was carving a small deer out of a piece of wood. He held the sharpened rock at the ready for another go at the deer's antlers.

"I have returned to home-time after each one of my youngsters passed through the ritual about one hundred times.

One hundred and fifteen winters, I believe. When not here, I have been back at my frozen-time protecting the time there. I go back every other moon or so to make sure things are not going too badly for the area. Of course, I could feel it from here if it were." He whittled at the deer's antlers a bit and then inspected the hooves. "It is not a daily war, as Eterili likes to make everyone believe. It depends on the area, the Manipulator, or Manipulators around the area. If there are Linears nearby. If the area is important to the flow of time. Some places are not."

Aithagg settled next to the old man. Once he began talking, he would talk until the sun came up the next morning.

"I remember when I was your age. I was full of dreams and energy and the power of the Vechey. Stay curious to have lasting power though. The madness. It took my brother, sad way to go. He did not come back for the raising of offspring even though he had a promised one with him. She was lovely. R'einla."

"Was?" Catha asked, curious.

"Oh, yes. She was lovely. We grew up together. My brother and I were twins. You see. Born at the same time. Well, I was two minutes earlier. Very rare for our kind. Difficult on the mother. R'einla, she blazed like the sun when she was a child. Crazy red hair that no one had seen before." The elder handed the deer to Catha, and she accepted it. He reached into his large front pocket and pulled out another half completed deer. He began to whittle again. "She only had eyes for my brother and I could not compete. They were promised and went off to the ritual as so many of us do."

He eyed the young Vechey with a wiggle of his eyebrow. "I suppose as you two will do too." He continued before they protested, "but it wasn't but two thousand winters that had gone by and my brother began to get disinterested in the Vechey way."

He stopped and took a particular interest in the eyes of the carving in his hands for a moment. His hands made short work of it and when he turned the deer over its eyes stared. "She came back to visit during one of the mating cycles, just to see my promised one, Fruana. They were friends growing up too, you know. Well, she started coming back more and talking about my brother. She needed comforting and guidance. What could we do?"

Aithagg interrupted with a question, "Did Eterili go see him?"

"Yes, she did." The man looked at Aithagg in surprise. "She visits us from time to time out there. Checking on her flock. We visit each other too. We do not stay in solitude. Some do. I suppose. Not all of us. But many of us. We are bad at time and given how we are all stretched out across the times—it is difficult to find everyone and pay attention to when you are visiting people. It is odd, all of time in our hands and we are bad at keeping track of it. After being out of sync with it—time does not mean very much. It is not something we keep track of after a while. Well, maybe some do. I try not to."

He fell oddly silent for a moment and began to whittle away.

Aithagg and Catha sat by his side and watched. D'olr picked up his story after a few moments had passed.

"It was a sad day. We do not discuss what happens to Vechey that die before their time. We recover from most injuries that are inflicted upon us. Cut our arm off, it can be reattached. Even mangled it will heal. Break our bones. They mend quickly. Rip our skin. It heals. Most all injuries, if they occur, can be healed with a day's rest. But the one true-death is to sever our heads from our spines. That happened to her, my brother's promised one."

He dropped the whittling in his lap for a moment, forgotten. "I did fancy her. Loved her even. She did not have eyes for me. I would not tell Fruana, my promised one. Of course, I am not stupid. R'einla was Fruana's best friend, so she probably suspected so. It was a Linear that killed R'einla and we do not talk often of that happening either. My brother could change time. He could fix it. But he does not. Eterili, I could go fix it but what would that do for her? She would return to a Vechey who does not want her. Of course, Eterili would have my fangs for thinking of changing time to fit my needs. That is not allowed. It is not the way." The old man looked at them both pointedly.

Catha encouraged him to finish the story. "What happened to her?"

"Oh." He picked up his whittling again. "She was a very curious sort, and usually that does good, but on this one instance she had followed a Linear to watch her. I do not know what she was so curious about. Perhaps the Linear was tanning a hide differently or painting something. I have no idea. Something a Linear was doing had caught her eye and R'einla followed her to see what it was. We all do that. Learn that way. R'einla must have been very excited by what she saw and wanted to get a closer look. That is dangerous. She slipped into main-time with the Linear. Well, that did not go over well and before she could fix her mistake and sync back out of that time the Linear's keeper cleaved her head from her shoulders as neat as day with a large hand axe. They tried to put the head on a pole outside of their tribe's area but it burst into flames once the sun came out. I am sure that fueled their fire tales for generations to come. I could never bear to go look. She died there and we could all change it but it is not the way."

He whittled too hard and the head of the deer broke off. He stared at it as it hit the ground. "Well, you have pulled a sad old story out of this old man. Let us change the subject, shall we? I hear that you garden a bit. Do you, young-one?"

She smiled and was hesitant to answer.

"Come on now. I talk of things that are not talked of. Surely you know that by now. I have been here since the first generation that lived through the ritual. I may have seen a thing or two. So tell me about your gardening."

She eased into telling him about her love for flowers and plants and the garden she was growing. The old man listened and asked pointed questions. He was curious about what she had found. What worked and what did not work. They passed the time until the rest of the tribe gathered round to talk about their evening's activities.

Vechey children played games and ran amuck around the older children.

Aithagg's mother, who had come near and sat down, eyed the old man with a raised eyebrow as if she knew he had been telling the teens things he should not. He eyed her in return. Both sat silently next to one another.

"Mother," Aithagg asked. "Why do you raise one child to ritual age and then return and raise another? Why not return multiple times at once and have them all at the same time? Then they could play and grow together." He did not add, for he should not have known, all sync to the same ritual time as well and all go through the ritual together. He would only know if he had been to the ritual site.

"That is a good question," Mother answered patiently. "But I only have the one room to sleep in. There are rooms here set aside for each of us. If I returned for all 156 children all overlapped, I would physically be here 156 times and need as many rooms. This cave system is huge. But not that huge to take care of me and thousands of other Vechey times 200 or more visits. Does that make sense?"

Aithagg considered it for a moment. "I suppose that makes sense. Time travel is very difficult to understand."

She nodded her agreement. "I do not think we know all that there is to know about it, either."

"Does Eterili?"

"I believe she is ancient and knows more than she tells us."

"She has things that hang on her person I have never seen." Aithagg looked at his mother. "Ivory beads that come from the tusks of a beast. And I should not know it but I have seen a small hard, clanging thing in her pocket. I witnessed her strike something with it once, when I was young. It made sparks like fire."

"Do you think Eterili did not know that you saw?"

"I did not think she saw me."

"If there is anything I have learned, is that Eterili only lets you see what she wants you to see. She tells you want she wants you to hear. There is nothing by chance with her. She has been around this land from as far as you can walk one-way to another and seen more than any of us. I am not surprised she has secrets. A very many secrets." Kei-tha tussled Aithagg's head as if he were five.

"Indeed." What else could be said?

The evening continued. Aithagg and Kei-tha had moved apart from the others, sheepishly looking at one another, trying to hide their infatuation and failing miserably.

Iskeho nudged Kei-tha and once he gained her attention, he nodded in the lovebirds' direction. She frowned slightly. He nudged her again and they both smiled together knowingly.

"Where we ever that young?" she asked.

"Younger, I believe," he answered.

The newly awakened tribe members headed off in different directions to feed for the night. Some together in small groups, some alone, some youngsters with a parent. Some carried lanterns. Many carried nothing at all, their vision having developed to see through the darkness.

Aithagg and Catha walked alongside of one another occasionally bumping shoulders and touching fingers.

Iskeho and Kei-tha watched the two go.

"Do you think they will tell us they are promised?" Kei-tha craned slightly to glimpse them through the trees.

"He will tell us before the parting ritual, surely."

"I do not want to see him get his heart broken over her. She may not make it through the ritual." Kei-tha's hand crept to her deep pocket.

Iskeho stayed her hand and held it in his. "If I could only have a few moments of bliss with you, I would promise myself to you anyway."

"You are hopeless." She tried to pull her hand away but did not try very hard.

"Yet here we are twenty-seven thousand years later." He kissed her hand, and they walked together towards a grouping of stone benches.

"A hopeless fool," she added.

"Always."

\*\*\*

Many moons later, the full moon was high above head when the tribe gathered around the fire. Eterili had not appeared yet, and many were restless. Tonight, the next group would pledge their oath to the tribe and to their duties as a Vechey.

Aithagg stood near Catha at the end of the fire. A youngster no more than the age of five ran past him and he jumped to get out of the way. He turned to watch him go.

"Remember when we used to play hide and seek?" he asked Catha. "Otski and Ygolz were always so sneaky about it."

"Is that not the point? To be sneaky?" Her smile faltered. "Speaking of sneaky—should we not tell your parents before we begin the pledge?"

Aithagg glanced at his parents, who both seemed to go out of their way to not make eye contact. "I think they know already."

"How could they?"

"You do not know my mother. You can hide nothing from her. She sees it on you as clear as charcoal upon your forehead."

He smiled and pulled Catha by the hand as he took a step forward. "We should do this properly."

Kei-tha was busy with a carving in her lap when the two approached. Iskeho plucked a carving from Kei-tha's pile and observed it closely. He looked up in feigned shock when the two approached.

Aithagg pulled himself to his fullest height and over zealously stated, "Father, Mother. I have something to announce to you two."

Catha stood by his side and waited patiently for Aithagg to complete his sentence. Kei-tha and Iskeho leaned forward waiting to hear the proclamation. Aithagg paused at a loss for words.

Catha began to interject, "We are pr…"

A gasp came from the tribe cut off her words. Eterili hobbled towards the fire pit. Her bracelets of fangs dripped blood as if they procured the well of dark fluid themselves. Red droplets trailed behind her on the packed dirt. Darkened dried blood covered her from head to toe.

Many of the elders rose to help Eterili. She stayed them with an upheld hand, making a "tssk" noise as if quieting a dreaming puppy.

All eyes followed her as she took her place at the fire ring.

Aithagg grabbed Catha's hands and pulled her behind him slightly. She did not protest and placed her free hand on his shoulder.

Eterili slowly walked around the fire pit, dripping blood as she went.

*Click.* The teeth.
*Drip.* Blood drops.
*Click. Click.* Gnarled fangs clacking together.
*Drip.* Blood dripping from ancient fangs.
*Thud.* Her stick resolutely plunging into the earth.
*Silence.*

Even the small children had stopped running about and ran to hide behind their mothers. One small baby began to wail inconsolably.

"We prepare," she announced. Then she motioned with her stick for the next ritual bound to take their place with her at the fire ring.

Aithagg turned towards his parents, his eyes wide with the unspoken words he had not had time to deliver.

His mother smiled and gestured with her chin for him to join the circle. "I know," she whispered. Her smile was warm and loving, tinged with melancholy.

Aithagg smiled warmly to his mother, then beamed a broad grin and briefly met his father's eyes.

His father was smiling from ear to ear. "Go," he mouthed and urged Aithagg towards the fire with a gentle flip of his hand.

Aithagg and Catha approached the fire hand in hand and took their place.

All stilled.

Eterili seemed to be without her normal showmanship this evening. Her voice was tired and gruff. "We begin."

The youngsters turned with their backs to the fire and faced the tribe. Eterili continued to circle them, walking, clicking, dripping putrid blood.

"What do you pledge to me, to the moon, to the sky, to your tribe?" she growled.

Catha squeezed Aithagg's hand, and they shared a brief smile before reciting, "I will go forth and find my time, my place, my home. Turning away from my family and my friends, I will dedicate my eternity to keeping the universe whole. Should another adjust my time, my place, my home I will defend it until my last thought, through all eternity."

Eterili stopped in front of Aithagg. She held out her bony finger as if to touch his chest as she had before in the white light of the ritual site. Her eyelids crinkled with a small smile that did not touch her lips. Turning she shouted with a little more gusto, "What do you protect?"

"Time." Aithagg's voice was quiet as he wondered what that encounter had meant.

"Why?" Eterili stood in front of Catha and patted her shoulder, leaving bloody smear marks on Catha's furs.

Catha looked straight ahead, afraid to move and answered with the others. "Lest the sky pull my bones apart as the tribe is lost across all of time."

Eterili moved on around the ritual circle but paid no further tokens of affection or attention to the youths there. She turned her back to them. "Will you survive the ritual?"

In unison, they hesitated then answered, "If I heed my teachings, we will survive the ritual."

"It is the way." Eterili quietly and with no further show walked away from the fire and disappeared into the darkness.

The mood was somber around the fire. Slowly the silence filled with uncomfortable chatter. A younger boy stood and with encouragement from a nearby elder he blew a trumpeting sound through a large animal tusk. A few of the youth, including Otski and Ygolz shouted and raised their fists to the sky. Aithagg and Catha raised their clasped hands above their heads. Neither spoke a word. A few more picked up the battle cry and shouted. Eventually the energy of the youths picked up. The crowd broke into its usual exuberance and celebrated the young adolescence and their ritual to come.

The celebration lasted late into the morning. Elders gave their best wishes to the ritual group. Many stopped to shower compliments over Aithagg and Catha.

"What a fine pairing to go through time with. You will make your clan proud, Aithagg," commented one redheaded elder who gave a large fur to Catha before walking away.

"I know you will do fine in the ritual." An elder male approached Catha. He was beaming, his grin nearly wider than his head. "I knew your father," he blinked, looked away, then continued, "before he came back and paired with your mother. We went through the ritual together, you know. He came back eons later and met your mother. When we were young, we tried to hide Eterili's staff. Fools that we were. She boxed our ears." He tucked a small pouch into Catha's belt then continued on with his story to a companion, "It was a freezing winter and we had snuck…"

His voice trailed off as he walked away.

One after the other, dozens of well-wishers bestowed gifts and tokens to the ritual group. Aithagg and Catha received an ample armful of furs and closed leather pouches.

"How will we carry all of this for our journey?" Catha worried.

"It will roll up neatly and be useful to us." Aithagg accepted a rawhide bag and a small packet of bone needles from a couple.

They fawned at Catha, "I know this is hard for you with your…" The woman stopped mid-sentence unsure of how to go on. She continued, "I knew your mom. She means well but can not…"

Catha patted the woman's hands. "It is best that she go on. I remind her of all she has lost and I understand. She cannot. Her spirit broke thousands of years ago."

The woman patted Catha's hands in return and then hugged her with such emotion the Catha nearly lost her balance. Aithagg placed a steadying hand on her back.

"We should go pack," he told Catha.

They bid their farewell and gave a last nod of thank you to the elders. In the cool dome of what Aithagg now thought of as *their* room, they began rolling furs and necessities into their rawhide bags.

Catha had nearly 25 small rawhide bags filled with a thin, hard something. She began opening them. One by one she opened a pouch, looked in, dropped it, picked up another pouch and then continued.

Aithagg examined his rolled furs; he did not need many, and did not notice Catha's examination of the small pouches.

"Look at this." She shoved a pouch towards him. "These are all filled with dried meat." She scooped up a half dozen pouches and held them towards Aithagg. "All of them. Dried meat." She looked at the packs of meat that would sustain her through the journey. Packs of meat Aithagg had no need of. Only a Linear or a Vechey with Linear traits would need such food items. "All of this time, the tribe knew? And they." She sat slowly on the cold, dirt ground.

Aithagg looked at the contents of the pouches. "This one has." He sniffed the contents. "Dried fruit of some type." He nodded. "Well, that takes care of some concern."

"I am strong enough." She looked at the pouches. "With the food and you helping me see through time for the jumps, I can do this. I can make it there to the ritual site."

"We have trained for this our whole lives." He kissed her on the top of the head and then helped Catha to her feet.

"Why is being Linear-like not talked about? Why is it shunned? If they knew the whole time and supported me, why not say so earlier?" She took a nibble of the fruit then offered some to Aithagg. "This is good."

He nibbled as well and frowned. "Not bad. If you like that sort of thing." He smiled at her. "Not everyone in the tribe is supportive or knows. The ones that do know—keep it secret. There is a stigma with it. A perceived weakness." He brushed her hair behind her ear to soften the blow of the words. "They will be far behind us soon."

They packed their bags tightly, leaving what did not fit for others to have.

Catha opened her small bag and looked at the shell one last time before placing it safely away. She patted the bag. "Ready?"

They walked towards the cave entrance and away from the only place they had ever called home, never to return.

# 16 JOURNEY

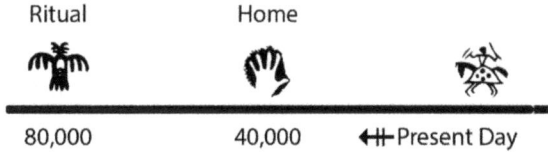

They set off, light on their feet, and urgent in their pace. Eterili still covered with darkened, dried, sticky blood—moved at the front of the group and set the pace. The trail underfoot was hardly visible, even by those who had developed their night vision, as it was a moonless night. By the time they arrived at the ritual site, the moon would be full.

Aithagg tried not to question Catha at every step, but his concern for her was apparent. "Can you see well enough in the dark?"

She nodded and seemed to keep pace well with the group.

He continued his enquiry, "Let me know if you need to slow down." He had been questioning her to try to gauge her abilities for the past four hours.

"We will have to get something straight. I am not a broken thing needing protection." She stared at him and deftly ducked a branch at the same time. "I cannot see through time, and I do not seem to gain sustenance from Linear blood as you do. That is all. In all else, I am as Vechey as you." She broke off a twig and threw it at him.

It bounced off his chest harmlessly.

They stayed apart from the group to talk freely. Otski and Ygolz ran ahead and stayed as close to Eterili as anyone dared. Occasionally, the group would stop for a small break. Eterili would walk amongst the group and eyeball the teens. Aithagg imagined she was looking for weaknesses.

During the last break she stated their directions, "When the sun rises, we will shift in time to the beginning of this night. Each sunrise we will continue to do the same so we travel all in the same moonless night. It makes us harder to see."

Aithagg wondered who would possibly see them: the tribes in this time were few. Vechey had very little prey being able to slide out of time easily to avoid larger animals. Even if attacked, their strength was formidable. He thought of Catha's distant relative being bitten by the lowly venomous snake and considered perhaps he was being foolish—an inconvenient attack by larger animals was possible, perhaps.

"When we arrive at the ritual site, we will join the others that have gone before you. I will lead the way to the time we will jump to. We all will gather in a ring together and step in with the group there. It is far in the past."

She stopped and turned to look at Aithagg. "There is a bright moment in time where you will need to follow me. You will see nothing else. From there you will travel to your own time where you will sync and begin your journey to find your own place in this universe." Eterili turned and looked at the others. "To begin your eternity protecting time." Those close to her shied away as she came near. The dried blood on her body stank of death and decay.

She moved on through the woods and the others followed. At first, they spoke and eventually they fell silent, concentrating only on their footsteps and the path in front of them.

At last, they stopped as the sun was near rising. The sky on the horizon, barely visible through the trees and brush, had a small streak of pink and orange.

Catha looked at Aithagg and without hesitation he looked through time. The rising sun paled the ghost images of the past and made them difficult to see. The ghosts were so numerous as so many had passed through this path over the thousands of years. Aithagg chided himself. He should have known. He had been this way and saw the cloud of ghost images marking the passage of the Vechey. He had to see through them to find a time just at the beginning of this night safe for Catha to jump to. It took concentration; eventually he saw through the misty visions and found a clear moment. There had been no one on the path then.

He thought to himself, if they all traveled in the same evening that kept the likely hood of colliding with other groups down to a near impossibility. Any Linear observing, if there were any around this time to observe, would see a constant group moving through the night in one area and a hundred other different areas at the same time as they moved forward in space but back in time.

This would not be a challenge after all. Aithagg bent and placed a small stone as a marker onto the ground. He nodded to Catha, and she nodded back.

The group disappeared from this time and reappeared at the beginning of the evening just as the sun set. Catha stood there a moment to see the orange and pink clouds in the sky. Then with complete faith in Aithagg she stepped next to the rock and back in time hoping she would not collide with someone from the group who had already arrived before her. She had not meant to close her eyes, but she had.

Aithagg touched her arm. "You can open your eyes now. You made it."

She gave a laugh of relief. "Well, that is completely frightening. Thank you."

They both looked around, and no one seemed to have noticed anything out of the ordinary in their behavior. After a brief embrace they carried on in their march towards the ritual site.

Catha pulled a pouch from her waist bag and nibbled at the contents when she needed and occasionally a teen glanced her way.

Aithagg glared at them if they stared too long. Ygolz slowed his pace to walk next to Aithagg.

"She eats Linear food." Ygolz looked over his shoulder at her then faced forward again. "I did not know that she was displaying Linear tendencies. Did you know?"

Aithagg mustered patience and answered, "What does it matter? She is Catha. She has been our friend as far as we have memories. Being slightly Linear does not change the fact that she is Catha."

Ygolz considered, then replied, "Her whole family is filled with Linears so we can not be surprised." He grimaced and picked up his pace.

By the tenth shifting with the sunrise, Catha was slowing. Her cheeks had grown gaunt and her eyes sunken. Aithagg looked at her with concern.

"You need to drink more water, I suspect." This trait the Vechey and Linears had in common. "Here, have my water. I will fill it soon. There is a river ahead of us."

She took his offered water-skin and drank deeply.

"We could pause and you could sleep. We can catch up with them at any time. Such is the benefit of being a time-walker." Aithagg placed the empty water-skin on his waist.

"I can push a little further. Then I will consider it," Catha answered.

She lasted four more transitions and then nearly stumbled into the river when they came to a stop. All sat down at the water's edge. Aithagg helped her sit down. They sat apart from the group. By now, the rumors of Catha's Linearness had spread and no one from the group came near them.

"Supportive group," she harrumphed.

"They are young and afraid of the ritual."

"They perceive me as weak and shun me."

He motioned for her to fill her water-skins in the river. He capped his full bag. It dripped with moisture.

"I will not hurt them. What do they think I do, eat Vechey? It is the other way around do they not kno…" She blushed with indignation. "They are not thinking of feeding on me, are they? Do you think that? I am Vechey." She sank. "Mostly, Vechey."

Aithagg filled another skin and capped it. "Your mind works too quickly that it runs away. No one is thinking about feeding on you. They just do not know what to think about someone that is different. They will come around."

She sat still and looked at him. "And you? Do you think about feeding on me?" Her tone was serious.

"Maybe a little nibble," he jested and bit at her shoulder.

Trying to stay angry she protested, "I do not know about eternity with you. I will pull out your fangs myself. I will bet that is where Eterili gets her anklets from—promised ones that kill each other from the desperate endlessness of eternity."

Eterili pointed at the river. "We will need to shift to a time where this river was not, then cross, then shift back and meet on the other side. Walking through water is like being cut with so many shards of sharp rock. It will drain your energy." She disappeared and then reappeared on the other side of the river. She lifted her staff above her head.

Catha turned to Aithagg. "Now *would* be a good time for a nap to build my strength back up. Everyone is shifting and we can sync right back there."

Aithagg looked around. "We will need to find a place that you can safely sleep and shift. I can stay awake."

"I do not always shift. Rarely, we have found."

"You can not sleep out here and shift through time, you could shift into the daylight," he added.

"I can take the daylight."

"You think you can. You have never walked when the sun was high above." Aithagg shook his head.

"Yes, I have."

He looked at her.

She continued defiantly, "I tend the garden in the day. It helps feed the young ones." She looked down and shrugged. "I will rest. If I shift, there is nothing we can do about it. If I do not rest, I cannot go on. Either way, I end here." Catha hefted her water bag and her pouches of food. "I'll rest and then you can help me shift to walk across the dried riverbed and then appear over there with the rest of the group. No one will be the wiser."

"You do not think Eterili will see you sleeping?" Aithagg looked at the group who one by one was disappearing.

"She knows already what I am." Catha stood and walked away from the path. "I will make it not so obvious and remove myself to a clearing away from the path."

Aithagg turned and watched the others appear on the other side of the river and trudge on. No one stopped to see if Aithagg and Catha were with them. He thought Eterili might have glanced over her shoulder, but it may have been only a trick of the dim light.

He helped Catha move back to the beginning of the night to sleep while he stood vigil in the dark. If she had stayed and slept through the day, Aithagg would have been helpless to come to her side if anything should go wrong. Luckily for her she did not shift during her slumber. It would be catastrophic to shift to a time where a tree was in the same spot in which she slept. The sun was near to rising when she finally stirred.

She awoke and pointed to a pile of small rocks sitting between her and Aithagg.

"What are these?" she asked.

"You'll know these when you see them. I carved them while you slept." Aithagg held dozens of rocks in his cupped hand, each carved with a small spiral and five dots around the spiral.

"What do the symbols mean?"

He shrugged. "I liked the look of it actually. It made me think of skipping stones on the water, but instead its time." Aithagg looked down. "Stupid, maybe."

"I see it," she said encouragingly. "The dots are the rocks leading me through time. I love them."

He smiled awkwardly not sure how to accept the compliment.

"Why does she hurry everyone so? They could stop and rest. The Vechey have no reason to be in a hurry," she asked in between bites of dried venison.

"I suppose it is a test of endurance."

"But anyone could do what we are doing right now. Slip out. Rest. Slip right back into the timeline."

"True."

Catha thought on it more then added, "Except, the Linears wouldn't be able to slip in and out. Only those with Vechey ability. So it is meant to weed the weak out."

Aithagg stayed silent on the subject.

She continued, "I suppose there are those that do not have someone helping them." She eyed Aithagg. "I am thankful and hate it at the same time."

He smiled and maintained his muteness.

She eyed the swiftly moving water for a moment then declared, "I think I can just walk across it. Water may not bother me like it does you."

Aithagg crossed his arms and watched from the shoreline as Catha dipped her toes in the water, then walked in until the water was at her ankles. A large smile spread on her face and she called back, "Actually, it is cool and wonderful." She frowned. "An upside to being a Linear, I suppose."

Catha took unsteady steps and tried her best to cross. The bottom was unsteady and the rounded rocks slid under her feet. The water continued to push past her and babble in protest. She held her arms out for balance.

"It could be deep," Aithagg called out as a warning.

No sooner had the words been uttered Catha's next step forward found no rocks for purchase and she plunged into the water with no time to cry out.

A splash and she vanished.

The heavy current battered at her and pushed her head over heels downstream. Catha curled into a ball and protected her head. A lesson well learned as a Vechey: getting one's neck broke, be one a Linear or Vechey, made a being dead. She bounced about on the bottom of the stream and hit rocks and sunken logs.

She was Vechey enough to not need to breathe. Ironic, she thought to herself, she was adept to water unlike Vechey. She did not need to breathe *and* she could experience being submerged. A sharp rock bit into her shoulder, slowing her progress downstream and she clung to it with all of her might.

Water splashed up her arms and into her nose. She sputtered as she took an intake of breath to call out. Clinging harder she pushed herself up onto the rock and struggled against the current to gain purchase. Like a turtle, she collapsed on top of the rock. Sweating and exasperated, Catha called out in defeat, "Can you help me get through time to where the river did not exist?"

Aithagg stepped into the stream and winced.

"You should not get in the water," Catha said hoarsely. "I can make it to the shore."

She struggled and tried a few times for the shore. The current pushed her further downstream.

Aithagg waded into the water, ignoring the searing pain and the drain of his energy. Sweat streamed down his face in pink rivulets.

Eventually he grasped her hand when she pummeled into a thicket of bramble on the shoreline. She held onto him and together they slogged to the shore.

Catha and Aithagg collapsed on the sand as one soaked mass regaining their strength.

"It is very deep in the center," she uttered in a deadpan voice.

"Indeed," Aithagg replied. "We may have an issue getting you back through time until that water is shallow or not even there. You can jump to a time you have seen if I put a marker in place. How will I get you to jump to a time well before you were born?"

"I suppose many, many little jumps. Like Ygolz did to go so far back when we played hide and seek. Do you remember how he sat there in the snow for so long?" Catha looked at Aithagg expectedly.

Neither one moved. Aithagg reached towards Catha's forehead and removed matted leaves, which stuck out at every angle.

"Yes. He did nearly freeze, did he not?" Aithagg answered. He kissed her forehead and together they proceeded back up the bank of the stream to where the Vechey had crossed.

With a little negotiation Aithagg led her back through time until the river had been dried with a drought. They were careful to choose a time none of the others had used. Once on the other side of the river they slipped forward in time and joined the others.

Catha turned back to glimpse herself and Aithagg when they had walked into the woods to catch up on her rest. She stared after herself for a moment. A sense of disassociation came over her. How odd to go in and out of time and see one's self, she thought. She did not slip through time as easily as the others, the experience was very new to her and she marveled at the surrealness of it all.

Aithagg was thankful Catha was unable to see through time as they were passing the area where her distant brother had died of snakebite. Later they would pass where another had dropped dead instantly, Aithagg surmised from starvation by the gaunt look on her face. He tried to not look at her. The features reminded him of Catha.

"What do you see?" she asked.

"There are so many images of past travelers here it is disturbing to see so many. It gets cluttered," he told half of the truth.

They continued on for the next 15 days in the same manner and without incident, though Catha needed more and more rest as the continuous movement sapped her energy. Even Aithagg and the rest of the group slowed their pace as they all began to hunger.

Eterili walked amongst the group giving them a keen eyeing over. Evening rains had caused the dried blood on her body to streak and cake. The entire group wore a layer of filth. She paused at Catha and looked solidly at her. Aithagg pulled Catha close to him and stood as if poised to come to her defense.

Eterili flicked her eyes toward him and smiled quickly. Then she turned to the rest of the group and called out, "There is a tribe in main-time where we are going. We will feed well. We will feed before we go to the ritual time. It is not much further from where they are," Eterili reassured them.

***

The night was still and moonless. They stood in the same evening they had started in. Conversations turned to wondering what a frozen-time must be like: what it must be like to be the only one moving, for shadows to not flicker, wind to not move, the force of the earth not pull things to it. Eventually, hungry and tired, they stared into the distance and whispered of nothing.

Aithagg leaned towards Catha. She was nearly listless from exhaustion. "You should eat. We all will feed now. I can see a tribe encampment up ahead in main-time."

She nodded her head absently and reached into her pack.

Aithagg watched her and realized the pack was empty. "How long have you been without food?"

"A few nights," she whispered.

"Do you have water?"

"Yes." She sloshed her bag, which was nearly empty.

"Come feed with me and there will be food for you at the tribe's campsite."

She recoiled for a moment then softened when she saw the hurt look in Aithagg's eyes. "I did not mean it like that. I fear being caught. I can not shift easily, remember."

They planned their approach to the tribe as a group. Eterili led the way.

"Beware of our hunger do not let it get the best of you. If you awaken a Linear you ruin the feed for us all. You need this to survive your journey forward," she said.

They approached the camp and stood in the center. Aithagg watched as main-time unfolded in front of them and focused so only main-time was visible.

Catha stood near Aithagg and tried her best to see but was unable to. The slight wind pulled at his long curly locks. Her own hair, straight and coarse like her mother's, was tied into braids at either side of her head.

Aithagg turned to her and smiled. "I'll place rocks along the way."

She smiled in return and watched him disappear. He wavered from visibility and then disappeared. A rush of air filled the void he left behind. Catha stared for a moment, defeated. A stone was near her feet. On it was a hastily carved symbol. It had become their symbol: a spiral with five dots.

She saw slightly around her in time, only a hundred years. A long Linear life span, she thought to herself. Ironic. All had left the night and moved forward in time. She stood there alone. The magnitude of her aloneness was as heavy as the sky falling down on her with all of its magnificent stars. With an effort she pulled up what last strength she had and shifted through time from stone to stone, following the spiral mark.

When she shifted into time next to Aithagg, he smiled warmly at her and pointed to a thatched hut in front of them. It was large and had an opening at the top for fire smoke to escape through. Hanging outside of the hut was cluster of drying meat and fruit.

Quietly she took and ate her fill while Aithagg disappeared and she assumed he went inside the thatched hut to feed. The camp was still as the Vechey move as silently as night, fed, and then moved back into the time they came from.

She hung her head until her hair covered her eyes as she squatted on the ground eating her stolen meat in the darkness.

\*\*\*

The group appeared back at where they had gathered. Aithagg glowed with strength and vigor. Catha seemed stronger but still diminished.

"Now. We prepare to go to the ritual time." Eterili herded them into a circle. "This moment we step into will be your last moment synced to Linear time. You will go forth and sync into your own time, your own moment, where you will exist for all of eternity. Your time there can only end if the universe ends or you let the madness creep in."

She stomped her foot upon the ground and her anklets clattered. "Then your very fangs will crawl to me asking for forgiveness. Do not stray from the way, and I will see you returned to our home-time to bond and bring children of your own into our tribe."

"It is the way," the teens recited, barely a whisper.

"It is the way," Eterili said with finality.

The Vechey followed Eterili back to a time in the far distant pass. Aithagg left marked stones for Catha to follow. They arrived minutes before the white ball would hit the earth.

Aithagg grabbed Catha's hands, and they walked towards the whiteness he knew was there. They were still far from it. It would be visible through the woods soon, visible to those who saw through time. He squeezed her hand gently. More than likely she did not see it. How to describe the white brightness of a sun hurtling to the ground?

\*\*\*

The group paused as the whiteness became visible through the trees. The inability to see anything distinctly through time unnerved many. Eterili urged them forward. Bits of hushed whispers hung in the air:

"Do you see that?"

"What swallows all of time like that?"

"Is it a sun here?"

"…a moon?"

"Can you feel that?"

Catha looked anxiously at Aithagg. "I can not see it. Only darkness."

"Can you feel the vibration?" Aithagg asked. "I don't remember feeling that last time. But I was far away and not on the path we walk now."

They all quieted as they approached the vast white ball of energy. It pushed at them as they approached. A vibrating wind pulsed with energy and made the hairs on the backs of their arms stand on end. Aithagg and others raised their arms to shield their eyes; the brightness was so intense.

Catha stared at dark woods in front of her.

Eterili's shadow crossed between them and the whiteness. "Come closer."

As they walked closer, the shadows of other teens became visible. They all stood around the whiteness, some scared, some brave, most wincing at the fierce glow. Aithagg saw his siblings, Catha's siblings (the ones who had survived the journey) in the circle.

All gathered around wore similar expressions of wonder mixed with terror. Except for Catha. She looked forward in bewilderment and sadness, not seeing what the rest saw.

Here they stood together in the past, all the Vechey who had ever traveled to this ritual moment. Catha began to look at the others, wondering which one was her sibling who would soon die. She touched the dead sibling's totem safely tucked away in her pouch. Aithagg tore his eyes from the white pulsing light, obliterating time in front of him, to follow Catha's gaze. Across from him stood Icaeph. He held hands with a young lady. Icaeph met Aithagg's eyes and they smiled grimly at one another. A moment passed and they looked back towards the center of the gathering.

The white throbbed and pulsed.

Aithagg was drawn and repulsed by the sight of it.

His body screamed there was danger and he should leave.

Catha's hand slipped from his grasp.

His mind wondered what would happen—how exquisite to not know and not be able to see.

He looked at Catha and reached for her hand. Fingers outstretched. He took another step forward.

It happened quickly, much more quickly than he imagined possible.

The whiteness all at once was around him, in him, moving through him. Aithagg turned to find Catha, his hand still outstretched for hers.

She reached for his hand, a sad smile on her face as she stared into nothingness. The pulse of energy did not shake her as it did him. It did not make the fine hairs on the back of her neck stand out as his did.

Their fingers touched and finally he grasped her hand as the time they stood in filled with a ball of energy. A shock wave tore through everyone and everything. Her eyes flew wide as she saw the whiteness as it existed at the same time she did.

"Aithagg!" she shouted. A bright flash of light blanked him from her vision.

He held her warm hand.

Shouts and screams were all around as the white energy pushed at him.

Her hand was soft, tiny.

At the center, Eterili stood, her shape dark against the whiteness. Her staff held resolutely at her side.

Pure darkness and a sickening sensation of falling backwards overtook him. Aithagg held Catha's fragile hand tightly until...

# 17 ALONE

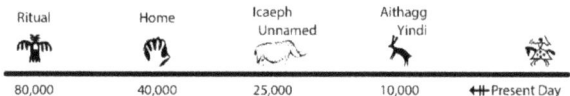

Aithagg plummeted through darkness and landed on his back. He looked up at the full moon and a sky filled with ice-cube stars. No white light. No pulsing energy. No Eterili. No Catha.

In a panic he jumped to his feet looking about for Catha, anything, anyone. The leaves and dirt at his feet drifted with his movements. There was no one there. Nothing moved. Nothing made a sound. The air was colder than he remembered, dead, unmoving. Aithagg took in his surroundings under the full moon. He was in a frozen moment in time. His time, he knew from his teachings. The whiteness had pushed Aithagg until he landed in his own moment of time. Where? Where in time was he?

He calmed himself visibly and concentrated. Slowly, the ghost images of the future in front of him came into focus. There was not much time in front of him. He was close to main-time. Maybe one hundred winters in the past if he was to guess. He focused then on the past and searched. The visions of the past were overpowering, even more so than at any time in his life. Having unsynced with Linear time, he knew from his childhood lessons, would cause his ability to see through time to be much easier and as a result be overpowering until he gained control of his focus.

An incomprehensible urge welled inside him; he needed to get moving again. There was one last thing to do. He needed to find the place where he would sync. Right now he had unsynced with time but had not synced into a particular place. He would need to find the place from where he would draw energy from the soil. A cave somewhere as shelter for when he slept. His cells would tune to that place and this time. Aithagg would have to hurry before his need for sleep became overpowering and he would die in the open, shifting uncontrollably through the energy-filled daytime. But first, where was Catha? A dread filled him. He had held her hand, the warmth of her hand in his and then…

Nothing.

Perhaps she had her own time. But that was not how it worked. When two Vechey were promised and went through the ritual together, they synced in time together. His parents had told them of their pathway through the ritual thousands of years ago. How could she not have come through with him? Did she get sent to her own time? Did she…

Unable to finish the thought he looked up from his frozen moment. Things were more clear now. The ball of whiteness was something that had come from the sky. It had collided with the ground and the force of the impact laid waste to all in its path. He followed the white streak of energy to where it impacted. There and then all of his tribe stood, had stood, waiting for the sky to fall on them. Eterili stood in the center of them all.

He saw through the whiteness now to himself and Catha. He had reached back to grab her hand. Held it tightly.

Then.

She screamed.

Defeated, he turned and blindly followed an instinct leading him north again. Numbly, he moved and let the dirt of the earth call him forward.

His feet carried him and he did not even care to heed the terrain or obstacles he tripped over. Aithagg moved towards a beckoning unknown.

Nothing moved. Nothing made a sound. He moved in absolute silence. Out of time, he did not even cast a shadow. The surreal-ness added to the numbness. It was as if he did not exist.

She had been there and then, what? Did she live in another time? Perhaps he should look. He turned back and a warm pain in his chest spread like fire as if the universe would have him correct his course. Ignoring the pain, he went again to where the whiteness had been; where she had been. Blood beaded on his brow as he concentrated. Perhaps the whiteness had pushed her to another time. He only had to look harder. She was in another different time than him. That was surely what had happened. He slipped through thousands of years of time looking for her, calling for her. Denying himself the closer look at the moment the white ball of energy had hit them and pushed him from her and into his synced time. His mind would return to the moment she screamed, daring him to look closer, to see. He refused. She was another time waiting for him to find her.

At last he resolved to see. He saw through the whiteness and saw himself and her standing there with the others. The meteor had rocketed from the sky pushing time with it and filling the void with its white energy.

It had pushed the Vechey out and away from it. They disappeared one by one. But not all disappeared. Some, only a handful, including Catha, cringed from the heat as molten rock crushed them all.

He dared not look, but he looked at the moment the rock impacted her and she disappeared beneath it.

Aithagg stood in horror at her fate. But what was fate when one could change time? He could step back and save her. Tell her to run, to not approach the whiteness. What good was this ability if one did not use it?

Eterili had warned against manipulating time to one's own desires. That is what the others did, the Manipulators. They changed time to feed their own need, and it changed the timelines and if left unchecked, changed the universe or could destroy it.

Aithagg turned his back to the image of her last moment. It had seared itself into his brain: her wide eyes, outstretched fingers. They had all stood there not understanding what the whiteness was. Unable to see the whiteness, she only had a moment to register the reality of the cause.

Pain gripped him. Jolts of agony pounded his skull. He needed to begin his journey before it was too late and he collapsed here in the open.

He focused on the moments when they all had approached the whiteness. It would be easy to slip in and warn her.

She was right there, had been right there. Her long hair in braids, slightly messy from the impossible journey she had just completed by his side.

The air was different, resistant.

He focused until all faded and he stood in time with his own self placing rocks on the ground for Catha to follow.

His original self looked up. "What goes wrong?"

Aithagg regarded his past self from only moments prior. "She can not survive the ritual."

Original Aithagg stood, rocks still held in hand. "Can I change it?"

"That was my thought. Lead her away from here."

The first Aithagg looked at the rocks in his hands and smiled a sad smile. "We had hoped," his voice trailed off.

"I have to begin my journey to find my home now. I will have to move quickly."

"You can return once you have gained your strength."

"Yes. Eterili will have us for manipulating time. I am not even transformed for a sun and a moon."

"Can we change it?" original Aithagg asked.

Aithagg swayed as a wave of pain overtook him. His vision wavered as if looking through water. "We have to try."

"Eterili's teachings. It is not the way."

"You have not seen Catha get crushed. It will change how you think."

"Why can I not see it?"

"After the whiteness, your vision changes. You can see through the whiteness much more clearly and see what happens there. It pushes us into our frozen-time." Another pain gripped him. "My time is short. I must move towards a place to rest."

"How will you know if I have changed it?"

"I do not know. We were such a good child growing up we followed Eterili completely and never tried to disrupt time."

"It might not work."

"It might."

"Eterili may stop me." Original Aithagg shrugged his shoulders.

"She may not." He turned and steadied himself against a nearby tree. "I must leave or it will matter not and I will die here exposed."

"Go."

Aithagg began moving in the direction his body pulled, leaving behind in time and place his other self who would try to change time, to save her. He longed to stay, see if it worked. He would come back after resting.

His vision swam again. Strange colors were coming into his sight. He had learned of this in his lessons. Strands of yellows and oranges came and went across his vision like misty clouds. They floated and seemed to be unattached to anything. At times the colors dissipated at other times they clouded his vision so much he wished to rub his hand across his eyes and wipe them away.

Pain and exhaustion gripped him harder. He pressed forward through the thicket, desperate to find a safe place to rest.

# 18 VOICES IN THE DARK

The dark of the cave entombed him. He listened to the distant drips of water, the air as it moved through the cave, the nothingness. The water gurgled and whispered. It sounded like distant voices taunting him.

*Everything you know must be a lie*, the distant water said. A haunting whisper on the cool breeze blowing through the cave passage.

Icaeph had not seen his Manipulator for so long now he missed the companionship. He listened. Was the Manipulator out there?

Silence. Nothing adjusted.

Time flowed, as it should. Peace for the world around him. There was nothing for Icaeph to do. There was no spear placed through the heart of a tribe chief that would start fighting between Linear tribes which he had to fix. There were no landslides burying a struggling, significant boar. Many adjustments the Manipulator made were inconsequential to time.

Some were cataclysmal in their importance. At the beginning of Icaeph's years he was unable to tell which was which and nearly exhausted himself trying to fix everything. Eventually he began to gain an insight into what each thing manipulated changed in the future. How did he know the things he knew? They came to him as images in his mind.

Or perhaps he made them up. A delusion? Icaeph blinked in the darkness. Stories he made up to entertain his own mind, perhaps? How would he know?

*You would not,* the voices in the distant water told him.

He stood at the cave's entrance in main-time, not remembering having walked here, and looked out into the grassy field. Small hogs rooted and grunted as they marshaled through the tall grass. A bird, startled by their progress, took flight and squawked its protest at being disturbed.

Silence and peace.

Nothing was wrong or out of place. If he walked and searched, he would find nothing tinged yellow or red as things appeared when manipulated.

Where was his Manipulator? Last placed in a deer—he would have killed the deer by now near a tribe, near a human host.

Icaeph missed his Manipulator. He had never bothered to give it a name. The Manipulator had never stated he had one. Where did this evil spirit come from? Why did they exist?

*It is the way,* the insistent hiss was much closer than the distant water.

Icaeph turned expecting to see someone whispering in his ear.

There was no one. Only darkness.

A wind picked up outside and the falling leaves barraged the damp ground. The hogs grunted and moved further away from Icaeph. They continued deeper into the woods searching for something known only to them.

In truth, he was bored. Had Eterili not warned they should keep themselves modern, keep learning from the Linears, keep moving, lest idleness bring with it madness?

*Hehehhehehehe,* the rocks laughed at him.

Icaeph glared at them half-heartedly.

Had he not just watched a tribe a few valleys from his own testing a new method of melting and pounding copper points? Other tested the properties of combining sulfates and minerals. All these things would be lost to history.

*Is that the sun? The sun. The sun? The sun.* More laughter fell from the leaves and jeered.

His body burned and ached before he saw the first pink and purple stripes of light in the sky. They peeked through the trees low, at his eye line, reminding him of his youth when he would stay out and try to see the sun rise with his friends. They would sit on the rock outside of their tribe's cave and do their best to outlast each other. He had always won at that game, able to outlast everyone as the sun's rays shown through the sky like shards of searing ice. Then he would have to retreat to the shadows of the cave when the searing pain on his skin became unbearable. His mother would scold him for the bloody sweat stains on his clothing that would need washing.

*The sun. The sun. The Sun. The SUN. SUN. SUN!* Birds screamed overhead as they took flight.

A voice close to his ear whispered, *It is the way.*

Icaeph nodded his head in agreement and stood watching the sunrise even as every rock and pebble and cricket screamed for him to retreat into the darkness of the cave.

He had always been the last to retreat from the sun.

# 19 LOST

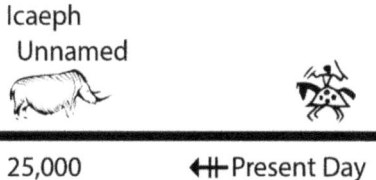

There was no peace. The world screamed at her from every turn. She tried to ignore it all but the incessant buzz of it all grew and grew until she covered her ears to shut it out. She had tried to stay with the deer as a host. Actively trying to deny what her instinct told her, drove her to do. She willed herself to die, to be free, to hear silence for once. What was that like? Silence? Stillness? No need driving her to change, to move, to manipulate, to molest the surrounding timeline. What was it to not crave destruction of everything? Did peace exist?

She did not remember before. Had she always been this ethereal thing that floated from host to host?

She did not remember her name. Her only name was her need to manipulate time. The Manipulator. She had always been; she thought. Or did she have a name before? What was before?

She thought of herself as she. It was the only image she had. Had she believed one of her own lies for so many thousands of winters that it had become true or near enough to the truth.

Not one to think ahead or dwell on the past, the next need to destroy would abolish this short-lived moment of introspection.

The sun was high. It tried to take the chill off of the damp air, but failed.

Her host body—now mostly useless and failing of energy already—sat listless against a stone karst. The uneven rocks bit into her host's shoulders and back. She accepted the pain, using it to keep her mind focused, if only to simply prove she still existed.

# 20 EXHAUSTION

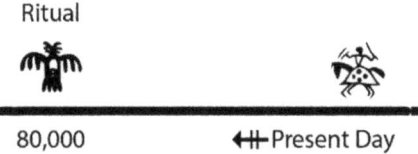

Aithagg was unsure how far he had syncing in the night to stay away from the sun. He trudged through the swamps; the snakes avoiding him as he sloshed through. The mud sucked greedily at his rawhide sandals. The sandals did little to protect his feet where everything tried to rip at the skin. While animals ignored the Vechey, the undergrowth was less discerning.

The air was humid and damp while still being cold. His already chilled body did not experience the cold as much as a Linear would.

Aithagg stopped in mid-stride and looked over his shoulder. He wondered where Catha was. Had his past self saved her? How would he know when time had changed? Dreams perhaps. When time changed, Linears recalled the adjustments in dream fragments. Perhaps it was true for Vechey. He realized there were many things he had not learned, had not grasped the entirety of, or mostly not known to ask the questions just yet.

A week of main-time later the soggy ground gave way to rockier ground with slopes and slight hills. He trudged through open grass fields and dense pine forests. The recent retreating ice and frost from his youth receded and there was more rainfall now. It splattered his cheeks and drenched his clothing. He had slipped into main-time and out of his frozen-time for the rain to fall on him. Exhausted, he did not care. He stumbled into a stream before even realizing it was there. It gurgled about him as he bent on hands and knees and drank deeply. Even as the water quenched his thirst, the running water pulled precious energy from him.

He collapsed face first into the water and with all of his might pulled his body to the shoreline. One limb at a time he hauled himself from the peacefully menacing water and laid himself upon the shore. In the darkness, he saw misty visions of himself through the trees. Was he going in circles? Or was he slipping in and out of time throughout the night? More than likely, it was both. He knew he had not crossed this water before. He didn't remember crossing this water before. His hunger was so strong, he was becoming delirious.

Aithagg eyed the fish in the water and supposed they might serve as food but lacked the energy to test his theory.

He lay and watched the stars as they spun across the sky. What would a lifespan of thousands of years be like? How much further did he need to go before he could sync into his place and rest? Then he might gain a grasp on staying in this frozen-time of his and begin testing his abilities.

Guilt hit him as he realized he was planning a life without Catha. Was he a coward for not trying harder to save her and pawning it off on his previous self? No one would live if he let himself fall asleep now. He could go back. He had all of time, Aithagg reminded himself.

The water babbled quietly. He knew he was synced in a time and he should go back to his own frozen moment. There he would be safe from predators and such, though they were not a large problem—they might cause harm. If given a warm-blooded

Linear versus a cold-blooded Vechey who did not exhale—the predators usually chose a Linear.

If there was a tribe of Linears nearby Aithagg could feed and would be stronger for his trip. He sensed none.

A noise caught his attention: slow, heavy footsteps. A large animal. Aithagg began to rise and shift into his frozen-time, what he was thinking of as safe-time. The sound was close and before he completed his thought of shifting a large bear came into view and approached Aithagg's supine body hear the water's edge.

Aithagg watched as the bear seemed unconcerned with the Vechey's presence and instead lowered his head to drink. The water rippled about the bear's paws and left droplets on his fur as it splashed. Heavy and slow, the bear walked through the water and stood next to Aithagg. It pawed at the ground a moment then laid down and with a heavy sigh, went to sleep. It was easily as tall as Aithagg and its shoulders were massive. It fell into a deep sleep, its breath rhythmic and slow.

Taken by complete surprise, Aithagg did not at first react. He blinked and stared at the back of the bear with its matted fur. Leaves, sticks, and perhaps something—Aithagg decided best left unobserved, as it seemed repugnant—covered the massive back.

An obvious food source and Aithagg was unmoving, too exhausted to react. He quietly raised himself to his knees and considered where best to feed from the hulk in front of him. He aimed for the neck wanting to be the farthest from the bear's claws. Be plunged his teeth in and fed. The blood was bitter but sated his hunger. Strength filled Aithagg's body. The bear slumbered on and never stirred.

Aithagg slipped into his safe-time and cared to not think about how the bear came to find him and sleep near him at this moment. Only briefly did he wonder at Eterili's earlier comment: she took the shape she wished to make the universe what she required. Could she take the shape of a bear? Or inhabit a bear like a Manipulator did? To preserve his sanity, Aithagg chose to not think on it. He accepted the event as it was and focused on moving forward towards the place that would become his home. He did not know where it was or how far he had left to go. The sooner he got there and rested the sooner he could return to save Catha or find out if his previous self had already saved Catha. He had to move.

The air became less humid. Even in his frozen-time the air had grown slightly cooler. The ground became steeper. Mountains appeared in the distance. There he would find water-carved dark caves in the stone. Was this where he was to go?

He would find a home there, he hoped, and soon.

# 21 THE WAY

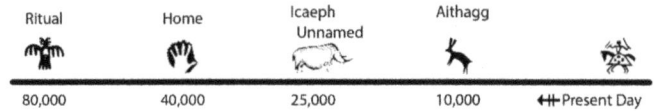

Eterili stood and waited. She kept the balance, tipping the scales this way and then that so the Vechey continued forward and maintained the timeline, harboring her secrets through eternity.

It was *the* way.

*Her* way.

The way *she* had designed over hundreds of thousands of years. Though she had been born many times, she remembered all of her lives. Many were short lived. She would return over and over into this world, this time, this universe, each time remembering her lives before. This current life was the one in which she had done most of her work, maintaining the timeline to be her way.

In this life, she had traveled the continents when they were nearly one mass. She and her siblings had emerged from her tribe as ones who experienced time differently than all others. When she had been born the nights were long. She realized from observing her siblings die painful deaths in their teens, she would be unable to walk in the day when she reached maturity. The tribe cast her and her mother out. They retreated to a northern cave alone.

Eterili did not blame the tribe. They were limited in mind and understanding. Her mother did not understand what Eterili or her siblings were and died a Linear's death in a cold, ice-covered cave.

The day Eterili discovered her ability to endure the sun was the day her Linear mother had died. They hid in the ice-cave as she became a teen and Eterili scavenged food for her mother during the evening. She watched her mother waste away, nothing more than a heap of bones and skin piled on a fur. Eterili, when she was young, watched her older siblings become intolerant of the sun. One by one, they had grown weak and hid indoors from the daylight. They had not been as strong as her, had not spoken or become aware as early as her. They were Linears in Eterili's eyes and she had learned from their mistakes. They were Linears with Vechey traits, that was all. Before Eterili and her mother had found the ice-cave, all the siblings one by one had walked into the sun and died. At first, they had burned darkly. Their skin split. Her mother tried to sooth their pains. They spoke nonsense, as if to spirits around them. Eterili, who even at a young age, saw through time and knew there was nothing there. They had gone mad. She took their teeth when they had died and created her anklet of teeth. From previous lives she knew who she was and how she needed to feed. Her siblings and mother were her primary food source, though they were none the wiser. She sat in the cave alone, after her mother's death and pondered what to do next. She had grown used to waiting. Eterili sat in the shadows of the cave watching the daylight outside. With a soft thump, a clump of snow and ice fell from the opening of the cave. This allowed the sun to penetrate the darkness and fall upon Eterili's arm. She stared at it fascinated. Her traits and strengths varied from life to life, but this version of her life was unusual. Stronger.

Eterili left the blood-drained body of her mother there in the cave and traveled further north and through the ice. She sought shelter in caves as she met others hoping to find someone of her kind. She found none at first. She had watched the world change and move, migrate and die. Eterili continued to move north and then west through the lands. She found one other like her—not as strong but stronger than her siblings had been. The woman showed the signs of being what Eterili would later name Vechey. However, the clan had badly hurt the woman for being different. Beaten until she could barely walk, they left her by the shoreline in a sea-cave. She would not join Eterili on her journey. Like her mother, Eterili left the bent woman, drained of blood. She had not even struggled.

Eterili migrated for thousands of winters. She had slept for another thousands of winters under the ice. She had called the Vechey from every corner of the globe to join her and they did. She honed over years the methods for teaching the Vechey, for giving them a purpose, and she understood the balance needed for the Vechey to continue to exist. She drew strength from them and the world continued in the timeline she liked the most. All followed the way and it was good.

\*\*\*

Icaeph waited for the sun. It was blinding in its energy and heat as it became visible in the sky. The heat seared at his skin as the intensity of all the energy that had ever been visible in that one place throughout time became visible to Icaeph. He cringed and fell back into the dark of the cave; its coolness was welcoming.

Sweating blood and panting like a Linear, he sank to the floor just out of the sun's reach. He saw the blue sky and the sunlight from the cave entrance. It was brilliant, horrible, deadly.

An anguished scream erupted from him and left him depleted.

***

Aithagg strolled through the valley and watched the full moon of his frozen-time. It did not change. The stillness was unnerving. In main-time the sun was rising. It pulled at his energy and sat as heavy as the universe on his shoulders. He pushed one foot forward and kept moving towards something—some place. He thought it might be close. The valley stretched in front of him. A waterfall gushed from the side of the rock bluff. It fell in a frozen splash into a small stream. Aithagg synced with main-time a thousand years in the future from his frozen-time. He drank from the clean water there. He looked at the waterfall falling from the rocks. There would be cave systems close by. He knew he was close. Perhaps it would take another sun and moon of main-time or even just when the moon rose and he would be there—his home. He would rest and complete his ritual. Then he would return to find Catha and risk changing the timeline, Eterili forbid it, to bring her here.

***

The Manipulator rested in her host, nearly dead against the rock wall. The water from the nearby waterfall splashed and the stream gurgled. She drank here to keep the host alive, but it was failing and dying. There was a small tribe at the far end of this valley. She should try to make it there and inhabit a fresh host. Unable to muster the desire, she stared blankly at nothing. In her vision the world was a sickening green, everything in the timeline was correct and she had not changed or manipulated anything as of late. To do so would have caused oranges and reds or at least yellow smears to cross her colored vision of the world. Oh, the ecstasy of those moments. The chaos and entropy of it all. None of that existed now. Only green. Only peace. Boring, plain, nothingness.

She loathed this universe, this timeline, and wished for enough desire to destroy it. Her host stirred slightly and twitched. She would have to leave it soon and find another host as she had thousands of times before. Having misjudged how much to push this host, she had let it come to die without having a suitable replacement nearby. Her failing eyesight and hearing barely registered someone walking and drinking at the stream until they were standing near her.

A man, tall, with long curly hair stood in front of her and looked at the valley. He did not see her. He did not notice the dying Linear with its evil host leaning against the rock wall. Her breathing hitched and she struggled to catch a breath in her fluid filled lungs.

If she killed this host now, she could inhabit this *new* host that stood in front of her. He looked exhausted but strong. Very strong. Too strong. She blinked and tried to focus her vision, which was like looking through a tunnel. He had appeared out of thin air, had he not? He was a Vechey. Just like the one she had tormented for these eons. A Vechey. She found new strength and roused the host's body for one final push. What a strong and amazing host a Vechey's body would be. She stumbled forward and the host's body let out a low growl.

\*\*\*

Unaware of the Manipulator shambling behind him, Aithagg pressed forward. He walked from the streambed and followed the base of the rock hillside. It bent to the left and he followed. Large rock outcroppings marred the terrain. Occasionally through time he glimpsed ghosts of Linears as they walked this way in the future. There must be a pass at the end of the valley in front of him. He continued to branch left into a smaller cove.

He found a smaller stream and decided to not cross it. Aithagg stood and surveyed the length of the cove where the stream continued. Hunger pains stabbed at him. He would need to feed soon. He urgently needed to rest. His eyes drooped and his feet moved like solid rock. The ache to move forward pulled at him like an invisible hand. He walked along the stream and went deeper into the cove.

\*\*\*

Eterili approached the cave entrance and looked at Icaeph sprawled upon the ground just out of reach of the sun. He blinked at her, not recognizing her face at first. Or perhaps not realizing she was not something conjured by his mad brain.

Icaeph was transfixed then jerked, his limbs twitching with the effort of him trying to speak. "Eterili," he whispered.

She clicked her tongue at him and placed a hand upon his shoulder.

He babbled something incoherent and pointed at the sunlight streaming in around her. "Sun," he croaked. He spoke in an ancient language learned from an elder.

Icaeph barely remembered the elder—a stooped, dark-skinned, wide-jawed elder who had come from a very far land, even further than Eterili. Icaeph, as his mind had degraded, had taken to speaking with the imagined elder in his ancient language.

"Yindi," he said again, in this old language the word meant *sun*.

She clicked her tongue at him again. "I release you from this place." She squatted near him and her knees popped loudly. "Go now to your next circle."

Icaeph was incoherent and his eyes rolled back showing only the whites. He mumbled, "Yindi," once more and stilled.

Eterili grabbed his skull with both of her hands in a strong grasp. Icaeph's eyes popped open, wide and startled. He started to scream. No words came out—only a garbled cry. She held his head tightly; the flesh indented under her fingers. Eterili removed a hand from Icaeph's head and deftly took the anklet from her foot and plunged the many fangs into his wide eyes. His screams echoed into nowhere. They had slipped into his frozen-time and the blood oozing from his wounds sprayed up as if gravity had less effect on them. The blood drenched both Eterili and the sixth lost child of Iskeho and Kei-tha.

She swiped at his throat with the fangs. A ragged swatch of flesh tore open. He gurgled, then stilled.

"It is the way," she whispered sadly.

She reached towards his mouth with her gnarled fingers and pulled his fangs out with a crunch. She took the time to weave them into her ancient anklet of mad Vechey teeth. They clicked in place next to the others. All those souls she had dispatched, freeing them to their next existence.

A freedom denied to her.

\*\*\*

The Manipulator came closer to Aithagg. She moved her host's feet quietly, though it threatened to drop dead with every movement she forced it to take. The Vechey was stooped in front of her, weak and kneeling in the dirt. She stood three steps behind him. It would be bliss to inhabit a Vechey. Immortal power. She would have the ability to destroy everything. No one to correct the wrongs she made. She was on the brink of freedom from pain, freedom from everything. Destroy the timeline and be free from it once and for all.

He had stopped ahead of her; she assumed to gather his strength. The climb up the hillside was steep and the ground gave way with each step. The Vechey was climbing towards the clear-cut area near the cave. Did this Vechey know the other Vechey was there? She had never seen two Vechey together. Only the one had been her companion of sorts for these years. His mind had been failing in these past thousand winters.

She saw this new Vechey stumble and thought this would be her chance. She lunged forward to attack.

\*\*\*

Aithagg climbed higher, grabbing any stick or root to pull himself up the hillside as the loose rock crumbled under his feet.

His vision narrowed to pinpricks in front of him. His hearing shut down. He would not make it to a safe place to rest. He would die out here in the open. Aithagg thought of Catha and pushed further. Pulling. Stepping. Dragging himself higher towards a destination his gut said was the correct place. Small rocks dug at his skin. Grit stuck under his fingernails. Bramble and thorns tore at his feet. Bloody cuts dripped. Blood-sweat mixed with tan mud.

Something hit him and he twisted to throw off the assailant, unable to see them in his limited vision.

The assailant hit him again from the side with a strength less than his own, even in his diminished state.

Aithagg lashed out with a grunt and pushed the unseen assailant into a nearby tree.

They exhaled a cry and crumpled to the ground.

He climbed further and came to a flat area, a small grassy level field. Here Aithagg stood. At the other end of the clearing he saw the rock-face of a hill and the opening he sought.

He neared the entrance to the cave and tried to observe it cautiously. Still synced with time, the wind from the cave chilled his skin slightly. He needed to find an earth source, *his* earth source. When synced, it would sustain him and give him energy. He was near his end without it.

Aithagg stepped into the darkness of the cave.

She pulled herself from the base of the tree. Arms, twisted at awkward angles with bone protruding from skin, hung uselessly at her side. A battle cry erupted from her chest as she screamed and ran towards the Vechey as he stepped into the darkness of the cave.

The earth welcome Aithagg and pulled him into the cave. A homecoming. Every cell of his body aligned with the place and the time and he finished his syncing. His body sucked greedily at the energy from the earth. He fell flat onto the earth, letting as much flesh as he had available touch the dirt to enable the exchange.

She was near him now. She only needed to be near him when this host died to take over his body. The power she would possess. She looked to see if her Vechey was near. He would pose a threat if he caught her. He was nowhere to be seen. This caused her to pause. In her weakened state, she had not noticed the nothingness of him. How could that be? Then she saw the new Vechey's collapsed form on the ground. She reached forward a hand to grasp him.

His mud-stained, sandaled foot stuck out of the darkness of the cave. She grabbed it with all of her might.

Aithagg opened his shirt so more skin contacted the dirt. His body breathed in the energy the earth of this cave afforded him. Something touched his foot just as he synced completely with the earth of the cave and his own timeline 1,000 years before main-time. A white shock wave rocked his body. Then the air became still and his shadow disappeared.

Her hand grasped nothing but dirt. The new Vechey had disappeared.

\*\*\*

Eterili knelt in front of Icaeph, years before main-time, his blood spurting on her face in warm streams and said, "It is the way."

A shock wave moved through the Manipulator and her host breathed its last breath. She released from the host and from all things holding her to this timeline. For once she had no need to destroy, no demands drawing her towards manipulating, destructing. Instead there was only peace. Numbness. Quiet. Passing into another plane. Brightness. Pure white.

***

A searing pain surged through him as his soul oozed from his eyes. Icaeph floated above his body where Eterili kneeled. She slashed the body's throat. He expected to be overcome with remorse, but was not. Instead he was awash with peace. A release. A floating. A calmness. His being pulled forward towards something, he did not know what.

## 22 HERE AND THERE

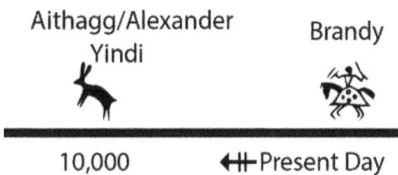

Alexander finished with a last coat of linseed oil on the bedpost. When he stepped back into time and caught Brandy as she fell, he would have to explain to her all he was, all he had been. As a Linear—a modern Linear used to electricity, connection to everything, and a facade of science that tried to explain everything—could she even grasp something so different from her world? Not just something—someone. Him.

Alexander smirked. He was the outcast now, was he not? Looking for someone to accept him as he was. Perhaps he had placed himself in this situation repeatedly to atone?

Alexander began assembling the bed pieces together. Each groove fit in perfectly with the opposing notch carved in the wood. He tested it for strength. It held.

He thought back to his first winter in this cave, eons before he had climbed up and built this house, more eons before Brandy had crawled into his cave as an explorer and he had fallen in love with her.

\*\*\*

Main-time's first winter in his cave where he had newly synced had been difficult at first. He had barely enough strength to move, let alone to travel and feed. It had taken over a winter for him to gain strength enough to consider what to do about Catha. His previous self must not have saved her. No dreams came to him as fragmented changes of time. No wisps of memory to show how things had changed. He sat against the stone wall of the cave and marveled at the stillness of everything, his isolation and disconnection. Disconnected from all things that had happened before. Even Catha was distant from him now. He was ashamed to think it. The whiteness and the ritual were a distant dream. Yet, he was more connected with the soil, the dirt, the place as if he was one with it. He supposed he was. The ritual pushed him into a frozen-time and when he came to this place, his body became one with it and was removed from everything else.

He existed in a smallest moment of time but saw no vision of himself as he moved through the cave. No previous selves, no future selves as he had moved through timelines. Only here. He thought back to Eterili coming out of the whiteness and there had only been one image of her. That must be her time. It absorbed her, erasing all other images of her through time. Yet she lived in it Linearly. It confused him. He thought on the vastness of time no longer. He was here and this cave was a part of him. Catha must no longer exist. It wounded him deeply.

Another main-time winter passed, and he had made it to the valley several times and was able to sync into main-time to feed on the tribes passing through there. It was a migration path, and the tribes followed the herds as they followed the stream to the river. He built his strength and by the time the green blooms appeared on the trees in main-time he was ready to go back to the ritual site to change time and save Catha. He had to try, even if it was not the way.

\*\*\*

Alexander patted the bed frame and looked at the bath nearby. The claw-foot tub, which he had brought back from main-time, nearly overflowed with steaming hot water. Brandy would not let that go to waste even if she did not believe him or did not accept him for what he was. He did not care. He had tried his best to save her from the Manipulator. Even at that, he knew he would fail. He had Brandy here in his frozen-time to give her time to heal before she had to return to her time. There she would die. Alexander was putting off the inevitable. She would need to return, eventually. He had tried to change time and save her. Time if changed too often will entangle and become white. Not orange or yellow or red as when the Manipulator changes things in time, but white: a hot whiteness locking time and events, making them unchangeable.

Alexander, now ten thousand years the wiser, remembered the first time he had seen the whiteness of locked time. Unfortunately, then he had not known what the whiteness meant.

\*\*\*

The coldness of Aithagg's frozen-time had become normal to him now, even after only one winter. He began the journey back towards the ritual site. It would take a moon cycle and he hoped to endure the trip without sleep. Sleeping in the open was instant death.

How comforting the first sleep had been after he had found his cave and synced into his place and time completely. He had taken the journey to the ritual site twice and then his journey to the cave. How he had stayed alive was beyond him as his exhaustion had been profound.

When he had first found this cave he had collapsed on the ground and soaked up as much energy from the earth as possible. It was something he had never experienced before. His teachings did not depict the desperate exhaustion and starvation for this new energy.

Eventually he had lifted himself from the dirt ground and crawled further back into the darkness. He searched for a room in the cave which had stayed open for millions of years. He had found a domed room whose ceiling had fallen hundreds of thousands of winters before. He shifted in time and entered the room when the ceiling was still whole. Then he shifted back to his frozen-time and the large breakdown boulders returned to their place on the ground covering the entrance to the domed room completely. The boulders completely encased Aithagg within. Safe. Protected. Able to sleep, he did.

It took nearly the full moon cycle for him to regain his strength and now he worried the trip to the ritual site and back would prove too much. He would be unable to save her if he was weak himself. Aithagg climbed down the rock side of the mountain and walked along the valley floor in the same migration path the short-faced bear would take thousands of winters in the future and the hunters would follow.

Aithagg had to save Catha, his promised. She should be here with him to help keep time safe from the Manipulator.

With one hand on a supporting branch and one foot suspended, ready to take a step over a large boulder, Aithagg considered. Where was his Manipulator? Was he not taught for every Vechey locked into time, there would be a Manipulator? The whole reason for his existence was to protect time. Here he was off to wrong time for his own good.

Aithagg had not even thought to look for a time being wronged. He had only thought of healing.

He was not sure what to expect. How would he know if time was being wronged? How would he find the Manipulator? It was not like the Manipulator would walk up and introduce himself, *Greetings. I am your personal Manipulator. See you next new moon when I begin.* Where did Manipulators come from? Eterili had never answered that question. She had only smiled.

Aithagg stepped over the boulder and his mood darkened. Questions. All he had was questions and there was no one to answer them or tell him if he had guessed the answers correctly.

## 23 ENTANGLED

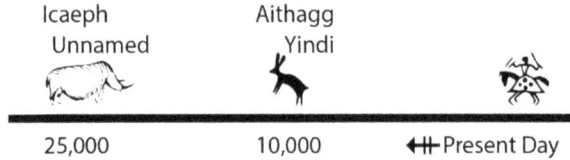

Leaves fell from the trees and the boy walked quietly so the razor-toothed cat would not hear him as he stepped closer on fallen leaves. The large cat dipped its head and drank from the spring water. Water droplets on the beast's incisors glistened in the morning sun. Closer the boy crept. Spear raised. His tribe would herald him upon his return. Perhaps he would not get chastised for hunting alone if he returned with a feast such as this beast would give.

A large squirrel chittered overhead as it bounded from one tree to the next. It stopped on a branch nearby and chided shrilly to the boy. He watched in amusement as the squirrel continued to convey his displeasure at the boy's presence. The cat did not seem to notice or care the commotion the squirrel caused. It dipped its head again to drink.

The boy transferred his weight from his toe to his heel until a twig was underfoot. He shifted his weight slightly to the left so the twig would not break and give away his position. His foot rested gently and silently on the leaf-littered ground.

The plump squirrel gave one last scathing retort and bounded away to places unknown. A small branch full of dead leaves dislodged and fell to the ground.

The cat's ear twitched. He stopped drinking, held his breath. He raised his head and his ears twitched and rotated trying to catch any other sound signaling danger. Hearing nothing more he stepped back from the water and raised his head. Ears perked.

The boy held his breath and raised his spear.

Droplets from the cat's chin fell to the ground, glimmering rainbows in the mist.

A feast, they would have a feast in his honor. The boy dared to pull his spear back further, his left hand held out in front of him for balance and aim. He would strike true.

\*\*\*

"Yindi." The word echoed in his being. *Yindi*. Why did this word echo in his soul?

He found no boundaries to himself only nothingness. It was beautiful. A nowhere-ness. So lovely. Floating.

The sun was rising. Energy filled the land and it soothed him. Perhaps he would dissipate and become one with everything. Or become nothing. Either way, it was a release and he reveled in it. He had been trapped somewhere. Where? A darkness. A misty memory, but this new freedom held promise, hope. He stretched or at least he thought he stretched. He had no form. No shape. He was pure energy, a life force. He floated and stretched and imagined the sun's rays permeated his being.

Rapture.

Below him the tribe prepared for the day's hunt. A small adolescent had separated himself from the tribe and was further up the valley, near the mountain's base, hunting alone.

Icaeph did not remember his own name or existence. He cared not and stretched further, the sun warmed him to his core. He floated as part of the air, on the wind.

Perhaps he would lose his thoughts and become part of the wind itself. He accepted his fate and relaxed. Parts of him fell away. The joy of the earth hummed and whispered. If he listened closely, it was more than the earth—it was the universe.

The infinite stars called to him and he wished to be a part of them.

Swirling into nothingness.

Release.

A sharp shapeless pain. A cramping of his dissipated form gathering into itself, colliding, molding, shaping, clumping, swelling, expanding. His being tore away from the peace, the rapture, the void. A force pushed him harshly and hurled him downwards. The sun seared his skin, hot and uncomfortable. The ground stuck to his face. Leaves cut on his eyes. A spear lay near his unclenched hand on the ground. The sound of a large cat, running away from him through the woods, was loud and obnoxious. A fat squirrel sat on a tree stump and stared at him, twitched his tail and then quickly scampered up a tree chattering at him the whole way.

*Yindi.* He thought. It was the only word in his memory. *I am Yindi.*

Trapped, he watched helplessly as his host brushed himself off, picked up his spear and walked dejectedly back to the tribe.

Yindi beat at the entrapped body and tried to take command of the hands, the arms, the mouth. Just to scream. Could he scream? He screamed. No voice emerged from the confining body.

\*\*\*

The boy raised a hand to his forehead as if a splitting headache had just come upon him. His steps faltered.

Rocks riddled his path to the tribe. He tripped many times on the way back towards his home.

When he arrived, he climbed into his hut. His worried mother, dabbed his bleeding forehead, then called for their healer. The shaman heralded chants and incantations on the boy's body through the days and nights. The boy became more distant and unable to talk coherently.

The mother cried when the healer told her the powers were not strong enough to remove the demon from the boy. He had wronged the ancestors somehow and they had sent a demon to haunt him. They banished the boy from the tribe.

He walked unsteadily, unable to bash away the voice in his head screaming over and over and over, *"I am YINDI."*

The boy accepted the darkness, unable to fight the voice further. Did the healer not warn him of pride and straying from the tribe's way?

The internal voice screamed once more, and the boy became nothing in the darkness, *"I AM!"*

\*\*\*

The trip back to the ritual site, the whiteness, was not as difficult as Aithagg had imagined. He had gained strength after he had synced to his place and time. He had not realized. He assumed pulling energy from the ground must have given him the extra strength. He had taken care to fill a small pouch of the dirt and hang it on his waistband. Even a small amount of dirt would give him some extra vitality during his travels away from his place. He would carry a small bit of his "home" dirt with him whenever he went on long journeys. He patted the small bag. It reminded him of Catha: how she had patted the bag where the small shell had hung, his promise gift to her. The promise gift, a shoddy reminder of death. Something he had taken from her fallen sibling on his journey to the ritual site. What a horrifying way to promise yourself for eternity to someone—by giving them a reminder they might die.

Aithagg rebuked himself as he stopped at the large river. The water was overflowing its banks. The ice north of him was melting. The rivers were continuing to swell with it. He was glad his cave was high up a mountainside at a false valley. The valley itself would probably flood in the next hundred moons. He hoped the tribes in main-time would be unaffected. Aithagg assumed they would be. The floods would recede mostly by the time the tribes he fed on in main-time took root. The receding waters would leave a false bottom of sediment on the valley floor making the climb to his cave a shorter one. He hoped it would not make his home easier to find. He liked the stillness there. The nothingness. No one had ever been there. Given his ability to see through all of time, he would have been able to see if someone had been there, or so he thought.

He dealt with the river by shifting back in time to an ice age where the river was non-existent. The temperatures were freezing, but it did not bother Aithagg. He crossed and then re-entered his frozen-time and continued forward.

What might have happened so his previous self did not save her? Surely there were a thousand ways to move her away from the approaching whiteness. Simply move the stones he had placed to help her through time so she was away from the impact zone. Appear to her in the woods when she rested and tell her to not go into the whiteness.

What if she did not step into the whiteness?

Then she would not sync with him in time and place. The whiteness would not push her with its magnificent, powerful impact through time.

It had not. It had merely—

—crushed her.

Aithagg knelt on the ground as the impact of the memories from his other self, his previous self, caught up and embedded in his brain. Being in his frozen-time the mud did not interact with him. The snake, frozen in its path as it slithered across the swamp, did not heed him. The tusked boar who might have considered giving a go at this potentially tasty though-unappetizing-smelling morsel did not move. The sky above Aithagg stayed frozen in its full moon. Forever midnight.

As the new memories flooded his brain, he saw what he had tried to do, hundreds of times and failed each time. Every single time—

—she entered the whiteness of the crashing meteor, reached for his hand, and the meteor crushed her.

—stayed outside the whiteness and reached for him screaming, but the impact consumed her, anyway.

—rushed forward and hugged him, full awareness in her eyes she would not sync with him. She whispered something he did not hear. Then she was gone.

—she pushed him away, stoic and mournful, a grim and tight smile on her face as the fire from heaven rained down on them, pushing him into his time and ending hers.

Over and over a hundred deaths of her filled his mind until his eyes bled. He sobbed.

Eventually his previous self, near death, turned towards the journey and barely made it to the cave. Now it caught up with Aithagg. He fell flat on the ground in agony—a hundred deaths replaying in his mind.

There was no passage of the moon or temperature change in his frozen-time to tell him how long he wept upon the ground. The tears dried. He ignored them. Did it matter how long he lay here? Did time matter anymore now that he was not a part of it? Aithagg brushed the tears, which had pooled and not fallen, from his eyes. Things reacted differently here in his frozen-time. Moved slower, had less weight, fell slowly.

He picked up a river-smoothed rock from the swampy ground and threw it. It skipped through time and landed hundreds of winters in the past. Curious he threw another stone it skipped hundreds of winters into the future, though still many winters from main-time. Sitting cross-legged on the damp ground Aithagg, like a small child, tossed stones through time and thought of nothing. The curiosity sated him and he tried not to think of Catha.

Eventually his thoughts turned to her and he knew he would have to try once again now that he was stronger. Perhaps he could shield her? All they had gone through to get her to the ritual site it seemed like such a waste to have it be in vain.

He walked on. In the deafening silence, he missed the sound of birds.

***

As he neared the site, he saw the trails of everyone through the multiple times as they had left the whiteness and synced into their own time. He did not see that before.

One image of Eterili coming and going shown brightly. Only the last trip of hers was visible as if this was her frozen-time. It made little sense to him.

Aithagg approached this whiteness again and dared to look at the ghost images of himself and Catha. All the time changes were not visible to him. He saw only the last occurrence, where she had refused to enter the circle with him and did not hold his hand. She stood there, stiff, resigned to her fate and smiled sweetly. His previous self had a look of defeat.

Aithagg suddenly recalled it completely. After a hundred tries, each death of hers more devastating than the last, it had become too much. They both remembered the iterations. Their memory of time did not reset; they kept each timeline in their minds. Catha had died over a hundred times. She had endured for him to try to break through. Now she stood outside the circle, resigned to her fate, unwilling to try another time. He stood still, defeated, and accepted her decision. She had whispered something; he hadn't been able to hear it.

Aithagg, in his frozen-time, stood close and synced in with the moment so he might hear her, 70,000 years before his frozen time.

"Last one there," she whispered.

The ball of white became hotter, it thrummed, and as it hit—

—previous Aithagg looked at her and then noticed someone standing next to her: himself. He smiled then disappeared as the whiteness pushed him into his time.

—now Aithagg put his arms around her in a reflexive, protective stance. He did not even think about what he did. He wrapped his arms around her pulling her weight to him. She had always been so warm. Her warmth touched his chest and he held her tightly. The whiteness pushed at them both and—

\*\*\*

The universe was hot, white, nothingness. It was a place devoid of sound, temperature, sensation—only the vast whiteness endured. Aithagg cast no shadow as he knelt on the solid ground. He dug his hands into the ground, scraping grit under his fingernails.

Numb. Alone. He could not recall what had just occurred.

He had pulled her to him. Her warmth. The whiteness engulfed all.

He stood slowly, unsurprised to see Eterili.

Before she uttered a word, he lashed at her with accusations, "Why is this place?"

She did not answer. Only a cracked smile pitted her filthy, blood-streaked face: a macabre, black-toothed grin.

"Nothing can change here. Why?" he shouted. His voice sounded hollow, the flat echo-less of it did not match the rage he wished to convey.

Eterili came closer and Aithagg took a step backwards. She stopped in her tracks and held out her hands. Rings of vertebrae, many with small bits of hide still attached, adorned her fingers.

She spoke, "Young one, you have an old soul."

Aithagg crossed his arms and waited for Eterili to say more. He did not care if he was being disrespectful.

Eterili smiled and stepped closer, slowly.

Aithagg stood his ground.

She caressed his cheek with the back of her hand, a lover's caress. The mottled fur from the vertebrae rings was coarse on his skin. He stood unflinching. The broken veins in her eyes looked like pulsing roots. A jagged rip marred the oblong dark pupil. Years of blood and filth matted and cracked on her skin. Her black teeth were jagged and broken into points, all of them, not just her fangs. He was surprised to see she had two rows of teeth. Dark. Jagged. He imagined green mold on them, the death of eons. The anklet of fangs jangling about her leg was less frightful in comparison.

"I am Eterili." Her breath was of rotten corpses. "The Watcher of Souls." She licked her cracked and bleeding lips with a fat tongue. "I am the beginning. The end. The Alpha. The Omega."

Aithagg stood still, his hands clenched his crossed arms. His chin dipped slightly, the only indicator he wished to retreat at least from the smell of her.

She continued, "I am the mother and father of Vechey. After traveling here and sleeping under the ice, I called to the Vechey from the ends of the earth. They came here. I found this place and brought—" She cradled his chin in her open palm. "—*bring* the Vechey here. I send them to their time to carry out their duty. To watch time."

She tilted his head, exposing his neck. Fear jolted through his veins. He held still despite it.

"As you get older, you will learn more about our ways, the ways of time, the ways of the universe," she added.

Aithagg interrupted, "Why do you only leave one trail of your latest coming and goings to this place? I can see all of my travels to the ritual site."

She smiled even larger and Aithagg regretted being able to see further into the gaping, double-toothed maw of death. He flinched slightly, pulling his chin back to cover his neck.

"It would be too much for you to understand now." She patted his chest and took a step back from him.

Aithagg hid his relief.

"The force of this meteor pushes you to sync into your time." She held her hand out and looked out at the whiteness surrounding them. "Me." She touched her fur covered chest. "I sync not into a time but into a universe and all of its time." She slumped slightly as if was exhausting to explain herself. "Though I choose this shape, it is not my only one. I move here—there. In this form—in that, to make this universe what I require."

She advanced on him again with such strength he took a step back and uncrossed his arms, holding them up in a defensive gesture. "Do you think I am so foolish to not see you try to save her over and over and over again? Like a stupid squirrel caught in a snare." She spat on the ground, a moldy red splatter. "Here you are again, synced and still trying." She went to beat on his chest and he batted her hand away.

"The whiteness," she sneered, "is an entanglement of time. Anything that occurs in it can not be changed." For emphasis she added again, "It. Can. Not. Be. Changed."

They stood face-to-face, noses nearly touching while she waited for his response.

Realization hit Aithagg. He crumpled to his knees and hung his head.

The whiteness seemed to brighten around them. It crept into his closed eyelids, seeped into his ears, and coated his bones.

Eterili placed a hand on the back of his head and croaked, "It is *the* way in *my* universe."

Then darkness began.

# 24 RAGE AND LOSS

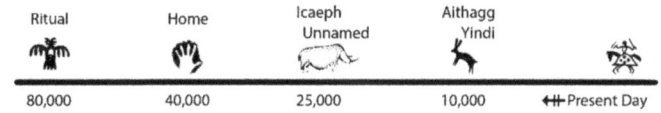

His limbs were as heavy as the planet. His feet as heavy as the universe. He opened his eyes and saw only blackness. Was this an eternal darkness? Opposite of the whiteness he had stood in with Eterili. He waited.

Nothing moved. He listened to silence. Having fed fairly recently, he listened for his own heartbeat. It was there, faint, but steady.

*Thump.*

*Thump.*

*Thump.*

He did not believe himself to be dead. He tried to move again. Whatever held his arms immobile gave way. He shifted and jerked with all of his might until one arm freed. There was a slight temperature change on his hand. Not much.

He was buried.

His hand now birthed into the open air.

Aithagg held his hand still, testing to see if pain would follow, if he was in daylight. He did not think so. Was it his frozen-time? He must not have been asleep, merely in a stasis of some sort.

Had he slept, he would have shifted through time and collided with all of this dirt. Though he supposed so long as he did not wake during his slipping through time, it did not matter. He would be the last one there and his being would overtake what had existed in that place at that time. The fear was waking up embedded in a stone wall, or a tree, etc.

He jerked and wiggled more until his other hand came to his face. Aithagg nearly hit himself when his hand broke through the dirt around his face into the small air pocket his limited breathing had caused. He continued pushing his hand up in front of his forehead toward where the other hand existed at the top of the soil. The work was slow. Dirt filled in the pocket in front of his nose and eyes but a new pocket opened up around his arm and hand as it dug upwards.

Aithagg rested. His body pulling energy from the soil. He must be in his cave then. This was his synced place—the only place where his body pulled energy. With renewed vigor he worked to swim his feet in the earth, causing the loose soil to open up beneath him slightly. The soil was not packed solid. The weight of the dirt on him was as heavy as his soul.

*His actions were unchangeable.*

He focused on his lower legs and wiggled them from side to side, using his toes to grab purchase on anything and "swim" upwards, while he moved his arms back and forth to loosen the earth.

*She had died a hundred times under the meteor and he was unable change a single death.*

Now he began twisting his torso. Aithagg was an earthworm churning the cold, dark soil.

*The last time, the 101st to be exact, the meteor had not caused the last death at all.*

His second hand cleared the soil and found the open air. It was his frozen-time; it had to be. It must be his cave. Eterili must have pushed him here. She was more powerful than he had ever imagined.

The whiteness had taunted him and he did not know its meaning. The whiteness made all in its path unalterable, unchanging. She had stepped back, after dying one hundred times and said goodbye.

*Overcome with sadness he had stepped forward as his synced, transformed-self and held her in his arms. The warmth of her on his chest was like a flickering candle's flame.*

Aithagg frantically wiggling, throwing his body back-and-forth. The ground about him loosen.

*He had held her, the warmth on his chest. The hot-whiteness from the meteor in their faces, causing them to shield their eyes.*

With his hands he scooped at the dirt above him and moved his arms in arcs, pushing the dirt away from where his head should emerge from the soil.

*Did he imagine she had looked up at him? She had turned her head into his chest to shield her eyes and looked up at him.*

Dirt slid back into the divot, it ran across the backs of his hands. He flung hands full of dirt further. He supposed the dirt flew through time and landed about the cave floor.

*Aithagg had looked down at her and the meteor pushed at him. He realized, a moment too late, it was pushing him to his frozen-time. With his arms wrapped around her, she would come with him. In unison, their eyes showed recognition of what was to happen next. What the reality of her hybrid-ness would do.*

His hand touched his own forehead and scratched it as he dug. He twisted his head side to side to loosen the dirt more and flung handfuls out.

*Aithagg and Catha had synced into his frozen-time together. She did not sync completely. Her Vechey traits were not enough.*

His eyebrows unearthed. He kept digging and twisting.

*In an instant, she dissipated in his arms. For a moment she was there, then she fell apart in a shower of small blue sparks like so many fireflies. Then his hands were empty. He had torn her into his synced time and she had blown apart into nothingness.*

Dirt clung to his eyelashes. He blinked them away. In his cave. In his time. Here. Alone. He ceased his thrashing.

She had been in his arms and then she fragmented through his fingers. He would never keep it from happening. The timeline event locked and would never come undone.

Aithagg thrashed in the dirt and swore at the darkness until his railings weakened and stopped.

His fingertips touched something on the dirt above his head. He gently probed, afraid of knocking the object into the hole where his head and shoulders were exhumed. His careful blind investigation found two objects on the ground in front of his tomb. He clasped them in his hands, not even needing to see them to know their shapes, and wept tears of blood in the darkness.

*\*\*\**

He thought of himself as Yindi now. Why? How had he come to be inside this host? A *Linear*. He knew that much. Yindi yearned for the freedom he had tasted before. He had been floating, free, becoming one with the universe and then pushed, forced, trapped inside this *Linear*. He beat at the host's head with its own hands and gouged the flesh from the cheeks in bloody ribbons.

Rage and anger permeated his body and he threw himself against the ground. Sharp rock shards ripped into his muscles.

Trapped. Trapped. He had to get out of this being. He wanted to be free. He *needed* to be free.

The body weakened. He collapsed in a heap—panting, filled with hate—upon the uneven ground.

\*\*\*

Aithagg finally crawled from his dirt entombment and lay upon the ground. His body bristled with energy in stark contrast to the emptiness of his soul. Main-time existed more clearly to him now. It moved on. The sun rose. It set. It rose again. Day after day marched on in main-time while the Linear tribes led their life. He mourned in silence. After many weeks had passed, he secreted the two items away into a niche in the rock wall.

Eventually his mind returned to his teachings. He had to protect time from the Manipulators. However, he had sensed nothing manipulated. The only manipulating had been of his own making, trying to save her.

In vain.

Brushing off his grief, Aithagg picked himself up off of the ground and walked out into the field in front of his cave. Here was his new home. It sat atop a limestone cap, which would one day be a false bottom for this valley. He saw in the coming thousands of winters to come the river would flood with glacial waters. Sediment would build up. He imagined as main-time marched on the waters would recede and the sediment would fill in the valley floor. It might even reach up to this cap where he stood.

For now he would climb down the rock mountainside and try to enjoy the peace and quiet. Nothing seemed to need his tending to. He suspected that would eventually change. He knew nothing more about the Manipulators than what Eterili had taught. Now he suspected she had not taught all there was to teach.

"You can not comprehend it all," she had said in the whiteness.

Perhaps in time he would learn more if he avoided the madness. Aithagg walked towards the waterfall at the base of the mountain. He had stopped there to rest on his journey through. He suspected it would become a favorite place of his. He synced into main-time to see the water cascade.

Aithagg, distracted by his own thoughts, did not notice the Linear.

\*\*\*

Yindi spotted him first. Not a full recollection, but a memory hit him like a bolt of lightning: Vechey. They had what he needed. Power. Not trapped in time, not trapped in these weak bodies.

Vechey.

Yindi's vision swam and a literal red swatch covered his eyesight. A growing need erupted in him like a flame. Vechey. He would have the Vechey as a host.

Blind rage erupted from him, rage at having his freedom torn from him, rage at the things unremembered, things rending empty voids in his soul, rage at the weakness in these painful limbs. Rage. Filled with an illogical need he ran without thinking towards the Vechey. He would—

Aithagg stepped out of his way and turned. "You are a surprise," he whispered and tilted his head.

Yindi fell to the ground, not having mastered the use of the host's limbs yet. He growled and spun at Aithagg.

Again, Aithagg turned and then looked at the path the Linear had taken. He saw the misty ghosts of where the Linear had bashed at himself and thrown himself to the ground. Could this be? Aithagg fended off the intruder with a slight push sending him sprawling.

Yindi spat the leaves from his mouth and wiped the dirt from his cheek. He smeared blood on his face from his mangled arms.

They faced each other. One enraged. One curious.

"Where do you come from, Manipulator?"

Yindi sat unblinking and frowned. He croaked, "I floated. I had freedom from this place. I was there." He pointed upwards to the clouds. "Rushing out into an expanse."

Aithagg briefly looked up to the heavens. The full moon had a halo of clouds around it. A storm would come soon.

Yindi continued, "Then I was here. Trapped." He held up his host's bloody arms. "ARHHHHHHHHHH!" he shouted as he ran at Aithagg.

Aithagg shifted into his frozen-time and out of the way of the crazed Manipulator-inhabited-Linear. He watched as the ghost image of the Manipulator in the future from him rushed through where he was standing and fell headfirst into the deep pool.

The Linear thrashed and his head broke the surface of the water. Aithagg shifted back into main-time and heard the splashing.

The pounding waterfall pushed at the Linear. He went under the water, one hand reaching up grasping for anything nearby. The Linear resurfaced once more and then the pounding of the water pushed him down again. The thrashing stopped.

Aithagg came closer to the water but did not dare touch it; wary of the pain and distress it would cause him.

Aithagg held so still even while synced with time he observed the wildlife come to the water's edge and drink. A small rabbit, thick furred, with large teeth, came near the edge and Aithagg grabbed it before the creature even realized he was there. It thrashed in his hands for a while then gave up and dangled, giving in to its captor. Aithagg did not harm the rabbit. He held it by its ears and watched the water. The teachings had been clear on a few points even if Eterili had hid many things from the young Vechey. Manipulators, driven by need, would go from host to host. Upon a host's death, they would transfer to the closest living thing. Except in water. Water held them tight to the dead host, unable to transfer while in it. Aithagg shuddered at the thought of being trapped in a dead and decaying body. Would the decaying body cause the Manipulator to shrink until it trapped itself into a fossilized bit of skull like a deserted island?

He held the warm rabbit to his chest, and absently consoled it with a gentle hand. He gently wrapped a thorny vine around the furry body, taking care to not pull too tightly.

The Linear did not resurface until the round moon had become fully obscured by clouds then sunk in the sky.

Aithagg picked a large branch up from the ground. Using it as a hook, he pulled the body to the shoreline. He waited, unsure if Linears could survive in water long, to see if the body was dead. It did not move. He used the branch to pull the limbs one by one from the water and rolled the body over onto its back.

The body, once removed from the water, twitched and spasmed unnaturally as if something from within was trying to escape, which was the case.

Aithagg placed the rabbit on the body's chest. The furry beast, wrapped in thorny vines, struggled to be free. The vine slowed its progress. It struggled, kicked, wiggled. Then it stilled. The beast's eyes turned back in its skull and it let out an unearthly screech. Then it began to spasm and convulse. The thorns bit into the rabbit's white fur leaving a bloody trail.

Aithagg considered leaving but was curious what this transformation would look like. He squatted upon his haunches to get a better look.

The rabbit in an instant shook and thrummed then began tearing about in a blind rage. The thorns shredded the skin as the rabbit now driven by Yindi wiggled out of the vine's hold. It bounded from the dead body and fell to the side as if disoriented and unable to drive its locomotion. The hind legs worked faster than the front ones and it fell over comically, pitifully.

Aithagg suffered for the rabbit he had sacrificed. Did it know it was being possessed? Could it still see out or was it gone? Gone like the Manipulator had been before? Dissipating into the above in blissful peace. Is that how the crazed Manipulator had described it?

The rabbit lay still on its side, breathing rapidly. If those small eyes could register hate, they glared at Aithagg with disdain.

Aithagg stood and slipped back into his frozen-time. He had met his Manipulator, who would continue to change time and try to defeat him. His duty of protecting time had officially begun. It was the way Eterili had described.

He looked at the body of the dead Linear in main-time. It was yellow tinged in his vision, something manipulated, but not a disastrous manipulation. How would he know the difference between ignorable changes and the ones needing correcting lest the time stream slip from its course? Eterili's teaching had left it at, *You will know.*

Aithagg synced with main-time and grabbed the body. He would hide it in his cave so the tribe would not find it. He did not need them to become alarmed. He did not want them searching this area, giving his Manipulator easy access to hosts.

Resigned to his fate. Aithagg hoisted the dead body onto his shoulder and returned to his cave.

He found a sufficient room near the back of the cave. The entrance to it had collapsed thousands of winters before, much like the domed room he had chosen as his sleeping chambers. Future Linears would not find this area of the cave. He shifted through time until the room was open.

The dead body upon his shoulder shifted with him. Being inanimate, it shifted completely and did not tear apart into time.

It caused Aithagg pain to think of shifting with a person in your arms.

*Her.*

Aithagg made his way to a dark rock room at the back of the cave. He did not know what brought him there, instinct perhaps. He gently laid the body onto the hardened clay where it would decay and become buried behind a broken wall of rock which had crumbled through time. Below the rock, had he cared to look further back in time he would have seen hundreds, thousands of bones jumbled upon each other in a disintegrated gypsum-covered pyre.

## 25 102

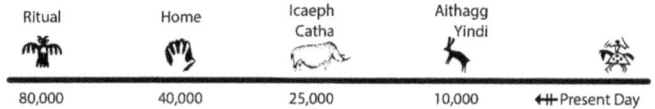

Catha had died one hundred times and kept each memory of each attempt at trying to shift with him through time. Each time she either stayed behind becoming crushed by the meteor or held his hand and tried to sync with him.

As the whiteness enfolded them, she had ripped apart into nothingness. Aithagg kept trying and retrying. He did not care if Eterili saw them or not. She held on for the sake of his determination, but eventually she knew it would not work. She would not shift with him. They would not stay together. She would die as a Linear either here or if she left the impact zone— starving and alone in the woods.

For the last attempt, she stepped away from him. Aithagg turned to her, understanding. She smiled grimly and thought of the games they used to play as children. When they would race and try to beat each other to the finish line. They would shout encouragement to each other. She would race him to whatever finish line there was. Perhaps there would be another place after this. They never talked about it in the teachings. She smiled a tight, sad smile and said, "Last one there."

Then, cool arms enfolded around her. Aithagg. But not the Aithagg of now who stepped into the whiteness to complete his ritual. An Aithagg of new. The Aithagg who had become, had synced into his time. He was different now. Stronger. Older. She looked up at him and smiled. She thought his embrace was a goodbye. She laid her head upon his shoulder, welcoming one last departure.

The whiteness hit. The meteor impacted, pushing Aithagg through time and his hold on her drug her along. For a moment she was with him, part of his time. The moon was full but did not reflect in his eyes: frozen-time. A fuzziness, like wet moss wrapped around her ears, changed to buzzing like a swarm of angry bees and then became the pinpricks she knew all too well. She began to dissipate and fall away. Nothingness pulled at her and she welcomed its cold embrace leaving behind everything.

\*\*\*

Icaeph, newly synced with his frozen-time, stood at the waterfall in a moment of contemplation. He had recently paused at this waterfall while trudging those last few hundred feet to the cave, his soon to be home. Exhausted. Weary. Ready to find a safe place to sleep. This waterfall had been an oasis to him.

He synced into main-time to watch the moonlight ripple across the water. The ripples crossing the water had always mesmerized him. The sound of an unsteady Linear approaching him caused him to lift his head.

She held a basket filled with berries in her arms. They spilled from the basket and she tromped upon them leaving black and red smeared footprints along the rock path. She was disheveled as if she had been wandering in the woods for a week.

"I was," she stammered. "I was there." Berries spilled. She pointed to the sky.

Icaeph stepped back slowly and said, "They told me of you. The Manipulator?" he guessed.

"The?" she questioned then dropped the basket. The rest of the contents spilled over her bare feet.

"Manipulator," he repeated.

She tilted her head to the side as if she did not understand the word.

She had been there. Catha yearned for it. Above. Becoming. Floating. Free. Though she could not remember her name. She wanted to return to that freedom. She needed freedom from this *Linear* body.

Another realization tried to materialize in her mind. *Linear.* That meant something to her. Or once did. She stumbled as she tried to find the meaning of what this body was. Why would the limbs not work as they should? She weakened. Did this thing, this Vechey in front of her have something to do with this? Had he taken the eternity of freedom away from her? Anger began to seep into her consciousness and eradicate all logic, all thought. A need crept through her. She needed freedom from this flesh-prison and the Vechey standing in front of her may not free her but would be a better host than this one she had. How delicious.

She screamed and ran towards him.

Icaeph synced into his time and walked away from her. They would have thousands of winters to play this cat-and-mouse game. First, he needed to feed. In his frozen-time, he traveled toward the valley pass where a small tribe might wander through following the herd. They would be few—but they would come this way.

\*\*\*

Thousands of years later, Icaeph sat at the opening of the cave firmly taken over by the madness.

Catha had inhabited as many hosts if not more in that time and had lost all sense of who she once was and what she once had been.

She stalked after another Vechey who was climbing toward the cave. Two Vechey in the same place; she wondered at this new development. Though she existed in main-time and the Vechey lived in another time, they would appear in hers when they fed on *Linears*.

The word conjured disgust to her, though she had forgotten why. The Vechey crawling his way into the cave's entrance looked no different to her than the other Vechey she had warred with for this near eternity. She did not know, could not know—it had been too long, this Vechey in front of her had embraced her once and she had torn apart into nothingness in his arms.

She reached forward to grab his extended foot but grabbed nothing but air as the Vechey disappeared. She screamed in a rage. Her broken arms ached in response. She stopped at the entrance and leaned against the rock. Her host was at its last usefulness to her. She would have to wander into a tribe's encampment. They would take her in and try to heal her. She would take over another host.

\*\*\*

Eterili wrenched the soul of Icaeph from his eyes and he floated into nothingness before being hurled into a teenage boy hunting on his own. Down in the valley a boy stumbled, not knowing he had become an unwitting host.

\*\*\*

Catha stood dazed and weak further up the side of the mountain. Something warm hit her host's chest. She looked up to see Eterili standing over her. The end of a spear firmly held in her hand.

"Child. It is time for you to leave this plane," she said. Her smile was broad and cracked.

A familiar prickliness started at the center of Catha's chest and radiated out. It expanded and released into nothingness as she floated from the Linear's cooling body. She looked down at Eterili who picked the Linear body up and placed it over her shoulder.

With a surprise Catha realized she saw through time, all of time, it was overpowering. Everything came back to her: the 101 deaths before the whiteness, Aithagg, the thousands of deaths as a Manipulator. She saw the connections of it all.

Freedom. Beautiful vastness. Everything. Nothing. One.

*There is no nothingness,* she thought. *There is only oneness of everything.*

Parts of her being stretched and tuned into the fabric of the cosmos and it welcomed her. Her last vision was seeing Aithagg come back to his cave with a dead Linear over his shoulder.

*I wonder who his Manipulator is?* she thought.

She wished it was her but was glad it was not. She could not imagine an eon of being pitted against him. That was not the promised time they had hoped for. Thoughts and identity were leaving her now. She grasped none of those things that had once been—so small compared to everything. She relaxed.

Warmth emblazoned every cell. She dissipated, with great relief, into oblivion.

# 26 ALEXANDER AND BRANDY

| Ritual | Home | Icaeph Catha | Aithagg/Alexander Yindi | Brandy |
|---|---|---|---|---|
| 80,000 | 40,000 | 25,000 | 10,000 | ←→ Present Day |

One last tidbit of carpentry work took Alexander's time. He crafted a small wooden jewelry box. He slipped into main-time to smell the cedar wood, if only for a moment. It was a good smell. The smell evoked memories of working with wood when he was a child and learning to carve. Memories of working on this house and building a place to live, something beyond sleeping in a cave. He had needed to exist, to learn, to thrive. Else, Alexander believed, he would go mad. He did not welcome the madness Eterili spoke of. Instead, he wanted to study, to grasp the vastness Eterili hinted at all of those years ago when he had gone through his ritual. He had reinvented himself a hundred times over, taking on new names and new interests.

The ritual-time, when he had lost Catha, still hurt: that loss and the many others that have come since. But losing her in his arms was an emptiness he still recalled. How long had it been now? Thousands of years? Main-time was in a modern era now with an infinite amount of opportunities to learn more. He recalled her warmth against his chest and then she was no more.

He straightened and brushed imagined dust off his pant legs. That was all in the past. But wasn't he going through it all again? He thought to himself. Here he had fallen in love with another Linear, Brandy. Yindi had jumped in to intervene. Yindi had tried to kill her multiple times. Alexander had saved her and adjusted time. Yindi had inhabited one of Brandy's best friends, spun him into madness and then used that host to push Brandy under a bus during the day so Alexander could not intervene.

It had only been a year that Alexander had known Brandy, but in that time, Yindi had stayed ever the vigilant Manipulator targeting his adjustments to time as personal attacks to Alexander and Brandy.

Alexander had tried multiple ways to kill the hosts Yindi had inhabited and to stall his efforts. Each attempt caused a worse timeline for Brandy and Alexander had witnessed an entanglement in time where she would die in the depths of a watery cave where he could not save her. The world had turned white, the whiteness, entangled time unable to change. It would. Not. Change.

He hurt so to think of Brandy dying again but he would not try to save her anymore. He had done that with Catha over one hundred times until both could not take the repeated tragedy any longer. With each death a part of his soul withered into dust.

He placed the jewelry box in the bedroom Brandy would first occupy when she would arrive at his home. The box gleamed.

Alexander stopped in the hallway, again returned to the portrait of Catha hanging in the hallway. A small shell and two polished rocks, encased in glass, sat atop a small square of bear fur. He briefly remembered being buried alive and touching two of those items with his dirt encrusted fingertips. Items left as a morbid tombstone. He tried to banish the memory and instead think of when those items were first exchanged as totems of love. The third—a stone engraved with a spiral and five dots.

"What do those mean?" she had asked.

It made him think of skipping stones across the water but instead with time. Now it made him think of time repeating itself over and over again.

***

Yindi had been quiet for a bit, not changing as many things in time. It was difficult at first for him, Aithagg guessed. There were not many things to change in this world where the world spun, animals migrated, tribes were hunting and gathering and some began farming. The most Yindi was able to harm were the Linears but was that enough to throw the time of the universe off track?

Perhaps. Aithagg was not sure.

Would moving one thing here cause a large chain reaction? If the Manipulators around the world all went unchecked, would they pull the timeline from its course? It was the teachings. It buzzed in Aithagg's brain, especially when he tried to poke at the nagging thought of Manipulators around the universe or even multiple universes. He thought no more on the subject.

Aithagg had slipped into main-time, tempting Yindi to approach him, out of boredom perhaps. He sat at the waterfall, one of his favorite spots. Small fish swam in the cold water and lizards with long blue tails crawled on the rocks trying to find warmth anywhere, left over from the day's sun, which had left the sky.

"I will not fall for that trick again. Drowning once in that waterfall is enough." Yindi approached warily.

They had been on speaking terms for a thousand winters or more. Rage is not sustainable.

"It is helpful to trap you in the odd rabbit so I can have some peace around here. You can not deny your nature to destroy things long enough for any respite." Aithagg smiled but watched his foe carefully.

"This host is new and strong." Yindi held out his arms for inspection. "I found it alone on the high ridge at the end of the valley."

"A lookout probably." Aithagg stretched. "That tribe will probably get wiped out now. I will have to fix that."

Yindi smiled a cruel smile. "Yes, I suppose you will."

Neither moved from their spot. Both relaxed but ready to spring should the other strike.

"You are more cognizant than usual." Aithagg poked at the ground with his toe. The leaves scattered and moved in circles. "The need will take you soon and you will not be able to hold a conversation."

Yindi stared at his reflection in the water and for a long while did not answer. Eventually he did. "It is a burden constantly being trapped; to rail at the bars that hold you in. I can only find escape in the small rushes of joy received from adjusting time. It is all I have." His eye twitched and his touched a hand to it. "The things call now. Those things promise ecstasy if I move them. Change them. The things." Yindi stared unblinking at the water.

Aithagg stared into the water at Yindi's reflection. "I wish that I could end your suffering, but see no way to release you from this mortal coil. Eterili knows I have tried."

Something caught Aithagg's eye in the water, a shape. Keeping a close eye on Yindi, who stared into space unaware of anything at the moment, Aithagg reached in to retrieve the item shimmering at the shallow end of the water. He ignored the searing pain in his hand.

Yindi stared in fascination at his reflection in the water; it rippled and changed shape.

The object was small and pitted but as familiar has the moon high above him. Aithagg knew it the moment he pulled it from the water.

A rock with a spiral and five dots. Catha. He had used these rocks to help her through time.

"Until next time, Yindi." Aithagg smiled towards Yindi—already lost in the voices calling to him. He did not hear Aithagg nor blink when Aithagg disappeared back to his frozen-time.

\*\*\*

Alexander stared at the portrait of Catha. He, at some point in his pseudo-eternity, had taken up painting and continued to keep his mind sharp, engaged to fight the madness. Even then, was he not at the brink of madness when he met Brandy?

He touched the glass case, the shell and rocks within. Did the universe not always put things back in his path? Tie things together in endless circles. He had often wondered about another level of Watchers.

Eterili was probably this. He was sure of it but thought no further on it. A mastermind, he thought. Then smiled slightly. An instigator.

Accepting the inevitability of it all; the fate of Catha, the fate of Brandy, the nature of Yindi, Eterili, himself; Alexander turned to go back to Brandy on the porch where he had left her falling. She would fall after tripping over a badly placed cat. He had to catch her and not let further trauma befall her. She was still healing from Yindi throwing her under a bus. He had disappeared from her time to better position himself to catch her. He needed to concentrate carefully to catch her without colliding with himself. He touched the missing piece of flesh on his pinky remembering the first time.

Catha's words echoed in his memory, "Last one there."

Hopefully he had prepared everything enough for the explanation Brandy deserved. With a determined smile he concentrated and slipped into time to catch a falling Linear.

\*\*\*

She wore only his shirt. The cast on her leg shone brightly in the full moon night. The cat had vanished, his malevolence completed. Brandy's arms had been about his neck and still were out in front of her. She stood frozen in mid-fall.

Alexander concentrated and carefully placed his arms out so she would fall a fraction of an inch through the air and then into his arms when he synced into time with her.

He knew she would die eventually, soon. He had seen the entangled white time. He knew more than most what it meant. This moment would be theirs and if she accepted him now or rejected him, he would bear the consequences. He loved her. It was his nature.

Alexander held his breath, though he did not need to breathe. He placed his feet and arms carefully and then synced into her time.

She fell into his arms. The weight and warmth of her hit his chest. The cast of her leg bit into his arm. He slowed her descent and took her weight into his body until she settled against his chest, which gave no evidence of being in a falling state. He stood solidly.

"Oof," Brandy exhaled with the sudden stop. Though Alexander had cushioned it as much as possible, it had still been a shock when mere split seconds ago she had been on a crash trajectory with the floor.

Alexander held still.

She turned her face to him, eyes blazing. "What. The. F. Was. That?"

Alexander smiled.

# APPENDIX

\*\*\*

Many of the events, places, people in this book are based on archeological findings. I have the podcast "History of the World" to thank. The podcast helped me see the full story and put my weird fascination with archeological digs and bones found in caves into context.

Here are just a few of such historical truths:

Chapter Three
- Eterili's mother is based on a Denisova jawbone found in "a holy cave in Gansu Province, China" dated to 160,000 years ago.
- "Tusked beasts shoulder-to shoulder" are Mastodons much like those whose bones were used as possible tools found in San Diego and dated as originating 130,000 years ago https://www.nytimes.com/2017/04/26/science/prehistoric-humans-north-america-california-nature-study.html
- The first man to respond to Eterili's call is from Australia.
- The small hominids that the Australian man comes across on an island are Homo floresiensis nicknamed "hobbits".

Chapter Seven
- Big-toothed creatures that grunted loudly: Castoroides, (huge beavers) which lived in North America during the Pleistocene age.
  http://iceage.museum.state.il.us/mammals/giant-beaver-0

Chapter Eight
- The word "Yindi" is Australian aborigine for "the sun".

Chapter Twenty-two
- The ritual takes pace at what we call the Topper site. This is a place in North Carolina near the Savannah River. Most artifacts date from the "pre-Clovis" time about 13,500 years ago. However, there is a controversial finding that dates artifacts also at that site 50,000 years ago. This is at a time before humans were believed to be on the continent.

The three circles represent the three stages of a Vechey's life: youth (Linear), Vechey who watch time, Manipulators who destroy time. At the end of their three circles they return to the dust of the earth and become reformed upon the next incarnation of the universe.

The universe gets recreated when its brane (membrane) collides with another universe's brane. You can look up Brian Greene's thoughts on the multiverse if you wish to know more.

The symbols inside the circles are the Proto-Sinaitic alphabet from 1750 B.C.E., which we cannot confirm nor deny Eterili probably had a hand in creating. This is her universe after all.

Finally, the concept of eternal recurrence, which is alluded to in the quote at the beginning of this book, was first posed by

Neitzsche in the late 1800s. This is something I came across while attending a lecture on cave-art after completing this book. I knew of Neitzsche but had never read his works. I think Alexander would have read Neitzsche. Indeed.

# ABOUT THE AUTHOR

Tina O'Hailey is a professor in animation and game programming, caver and occasional mapper of grim, wet, twisty caves (if she owes a friend a favor or loses a bet), whose passion is to be secluded on a mountain and to write whilst surrounded by small, furry dogs and hot coffee. Tina was once struck by lightning.

She has served as an artistic trainer for Walt Disney Feature Animation, Dreamworks and Electronic Arts. Any movie credit she has is minimal and usually found in the special thanks section. The meager credits do not account for the great honor it was to teach talented artists who worked on numerous feature films and games.

She has authored animation textbooks "*Rig it Right*" and "*Hybrid Animation*" published by Focal Press and the Darkness Series "*Absolute Darkness*" and "*When Darkness Begins*" published by Black Rose Writing.

You can follow her adventures here at
coffeediem.wordpress.com.

## NOTE FROM THE AUTHOR

Word-of-mouth is crucial for any author to succeed. If you enjoyed the book, please leave a review online—anywhere you are able. Even if it's just a sentence or two. It would make all the difference and would be very much appreciated.

Thanks!
…tina

Thank you so much for reading one of Tina O'Hailey's novels.
If you enjoyed the experience, please check out our recommended
title for your next great read!

*Absolute Darkness* by Tina O'Hailey

A thrill ride through time that will make you hold your breath.

Sitting by the campfire, Brandy admitted a secret to her friends. She swore she saw a ghost when exiting a cave earlier that day. Was she seeing things? Did they believe her? The next day, breaking a cardinal rule, she snuck back to the cave alone. No one knew where she was. What if she fell or was trapped? There would be no rescue.

For ten thousand years Alexander had kept the time streams of this universe safe from an eternal destructive force that continually threatened to tamper and destroy all. Locked in an unremitting battle, the two foes become sidetracked by an unexpected visitor. An entangled journey begins with chilling twists and turns until becoming locked into an inescapable death in a submerged cave.

View other Black Rose Writing titles at
www.blackrosewriting.com/books and use promo code
**PRINT** to receive a **20% discount** when purchasing.